The Seasons are Horses

The Seasons are Horses

Bernice Friesen

Thistledown Press Ltd.

Canadian Cataloguing in Publication Data

Friesen, Bernice, 1966-

The seasons are horses
ISBN 1-895449-40-5

I. Title.

PS8561.R54S4 1995   C813'.54   C95-920053-3
PR9199.3.F75S4 1995

Book design by A,M, Forrie
Cover art by Iris Hauser
Illustrations by Bernice Friesen
Set in 11 pt. Class Garamond
by Thistledown Press

Printed and bound in Canada by
Kromar Printing
Winnipeg, Manitoba

Thistledown Press Ltd.
633 Main Street
Saskatoon, Saskatchewan
S7H 0J8

Acknowledgements
Some of these stories have previously appeared in *Prairie Fire, Grain, NeWest Review, Prairie Journal, Western People* and *Ambience* (CBC Radio).
"Breaking Eggs" will appear in *Dalhousie Review*, Winter 1995.
"Living Dangerously" will be included in a forthcoming anthology.

This book has been published with the assistance of The Canada Council
and the Saskatchewan Arts Board.

. . . O fierce she was, mean and unaccommodating;
But I think now of the toss of her gold earrings,
Their proud carnal assertion, and her youngest sings,
While all the rivers of her red veins move into the sea.

Irving Layton
from *Keine Lazarovitch*

for Colin

CONTENTS

Breaking Eggs   9

The Monarch   18

Living Dangerously   22

Scorch   35

Laughing Buck Fagan   40

Kicking Down   50

Gabriel's Crossing   59

Ave Maria   71

Belonging To The Dragon   77

Brother Dear   87

Kelly Neudorf Learns How To Kiss   98

Teasing Boys   111

Musical Friends   119

The Sun Pushing The Wind   131

The Seasons Are Horses   140

BREAKING EGGS
Author: Bernice Friesen.

It sits on my desk in a sour cream container, in a nest of white and pink Kleenex. On it is a happy face, slightly screwy, and a squiggle of yellow marker on top for hair. The assignment is to carry an egg around for a week, pretending it's your kid. Dad could hardly believe it when I told him Mrs. Bowman makes the Family Life class do this every year. He told me to do what I want — even scramble it and lose the ten marks if it would make me feel better. I don't know why I'm taking this stupid class anyway. Just because Stephanie's here and everyone else is doing it, I guess.

" . . . and at this point, the sperm meets the egg."

Mrs. Bowman's flabby cheeks get redder and splotchy. Reproduction embarrasses her almost as much as it embarrasses Stephanie. Stephanie's only sixteen like me, so it's forgivable. Mrs. Bowman has three kids, so it's not.

"Can you imagine Mrs. B. having sex?" I whisper, and point out Mrs. B.'s bulgy panty line. Stephanie once told me I was the funniest person in the world. She's weird with jokes. She laughs the hardest at the dirty ones, but won't tell them; she absorbs them but then won't let them escape.

"Shh, Lori," Stephanie always blushes when she laughs.

"Our next topic is motherhood, the most important part of the Home Economics course," Mrs. Bowman says, right after she skims over the pregnancy handouts with us. She'd been sick, so we were way behind in our notes. I think she got sick on purpose, just so she could skip over the sex part.

I squash the new heading under the scrawled notes on my last page, and wish I hadn't been late for class so I could have gotten paper from my locker. I'd seen Stephanie, Lill and Faith whispering at the locked door, and when I'd got there, they'd stopped, guilty looks on their faces, especially Stephanie. At first I'd thought they were talking about me, but Mrs. Bowman was walking right behind me jangling her keys, so I couldn't be sure.

Stephanie stops drawing hearts on her pregnancy handout.

"You know, we were talking about you before class," she says, forcing an elf smile on her face, glancing up to see if Mrs. Bowman is watching. "We think you need a guy."

"I don't *need* anything."

She sucks her lips inside until you can't see them, and her mouth is a thin line, like she's thinking. She used to say I should learn how to flirt. I can't. You can't when you're sort of one of the boys. It's too phony.

Stephanie writes the word "Motherhood" at the top of a fresh white paper and underlines it neatly in red ink using a short plastic ruler. She's been my best friend since we were ten, but she's changed a lot. We used to have to do everything together — play catch, horses, pirates, explorers, then Stephanie thought she had to grow up. She started wearing skirts and makeup, and forgetting the fun things. Really, this is what her mother told her to do. Act like a lady now.

I've never acted like a lady, and I never will. That's because I've got something ladies aren't supposed to have: a good arm. I can pitch as hard as any guy in the school, and the rest of me is as good as my arm. I'm tall and I'm fast. Dad started me training in track two years ago in Saskatoon. I've already won a gold for the hundred meters at Provincial's, and this summer, I'm going to the Canada games. And people used to think I was crazy to get up at six AM to run. Dad says shoot for the stars. Maybe the Olympics one day. I've been taking his advice and trying everything. Grassbank is too small to have hockey for girls, so I joined the boy's team — a few of the jocks freaking out, of course, but Dad went to bat for me. He's the Phys. Ed. teacher here, and he used to play for the Saskatchewan Rough-riders way back when men were men and women did a lot of unnecessary ironing.

"The mother-child relationship is the only truly natural relationship," Mrs. Bowman spouts. "The mothering instinct is one of the most powerful urges of nature." The woman is flying now. If there was ever a motherhood cult, she would be the high priestess. I doubt my mom and her would hit it off. Mom's always complaining about how little time she gets to herself with me and my three fiendish little brothers. I guess you can't get to the Olympics if you've got kids. That's what my coach says.

"Oh, oh. I have this terrible urge to have a baby — right now!" I hold my stomach and whisper to Stephanie.

For a second, I think she's going to laugh, but then she stiffens and readjusts herself in her seat. I'm being disrespectful, I guess. Her mother wants lots of grandchildren. I think her mother is crazy. If you wanted a lot of grandchildren, why wouldn't you tell your only child about sex? Huh? Insane or what? When Stephanie got her first period, her mother showed her how to wash the blood out of her panties and gave her a big box of Kotex — the antique kind that you still had to wear with a belt. The only words that came out of her mother's mouth were laundry instructions. Stephanie was afraid to ask her questions too, with her mother never saying the words "brassiere", "panties" or "pads" above a fearful whisper. I had to take over on the sex subject. I told Stephanie all about it. She says I'm smart and I'm tough. I think she depends on me.

" . . . take the female bear. I'm sure you've heard of how dangerous she is when her young are threatened. Female bears must protect their cubs from male bears, who will sometimes kill and eat even their own young."

"Eww . . . " Stephanie whispers to me, but I'm not as impressed.

"Female fish eat their own minnows," I say out loud, being fake and perky, pretending I'm helping somehow. Mrs. Bowman opens and closes her mouth, then gulps as if she's swallowing a guppy. There's a laugh from Lill in the back and a lot of whispering. I glance back instead of taking a bow, and everyone is looking at me strange, like they're trying to figure me out. For the first time, I feel more laughed at than laughed with.

"I was talking about the *higher* animals, Lori," Mrs. Bowman sticks her boobs out. Old bag.

Stephanie looks over at me, worry lines between her eyebrows. She's not copying the notes Mrs. Bowman is putting on the blackboard. She's cutting a half circle out of a piece of blue scrap paper. She takes some scotch tape out of her pencil case and tapes the paper to her egg like a baby bonnet.

"It's a boy. His name is Bartley."

I point to my egg. "It's an egg. It's name is Humpty."

She laughs and laughs, hand over her mouth, and Mrs. Bowman gives her a glare.

"You can be such as scream," she whispers to me, and we look each other in the eye the way we used to when we were planning to cram newspaper into Alex the Chicken's locker. "I can never think of those things." The smile on her face goes still, sinks into worry. "We were talking about you before class."

"Yeah? You already told me."

She leans her head to one side and gives a little breathy laugh, as if apologizing for what she's about to say.

"We think you need a guy."

"Why are you so stuck on this? And who is 'we'?"

"Well, you know. Everybody."

"So?"

The bell rings. Noon. This topic of conversation better be over. I slam my binder, which now has Family Life notes written down the cover, and stand up, pushing the chair behind me so it vibrates. I pick up my stupid egg. It grins at me, lolling in the Kleenex I feel like blowing my nose in. I snap the lid on the container. Stephanie follows me into the hall.

"Rod likes you."

"Rod is studying to be the antichrist."

"But he's so cute."

I stop and look at her.

"Do you know what that idiot did at hockey practice last night? Asked me if I wanted to screw him, on the ice, in front of all the guys."

Her eyes go wide. She puts her hand over her egg container as if to protect her fragile white child. "What did you say?"

"Nothing. Nick and Mur told me they'd help me punch him out after, but I high sticked him once when Coach wasn't looking. Too bad he was wearing his cup."

She sputters and laughs trying to hold her mouth closed with her hand, her other hand holding her books and egg to her belly.

"OKAY. Not him. There are others."

We put our books in our lockers and take our lunches to the senior lunch room, which is also the social studies and biology room. It's more crowded than usual because, like us, some of the town kids bring their lunch when it's really cold outside and they don't want to walk home. Rod and Darren are sitting on desks in the corner, underneath the big poster of the food chain. Lill and Faith are in the desks beside them by the snowy windows. The only empty desks are in front of them. Great.

Rod watches me, swinging his long legs slowly, the way a cat twitches it's tail. He's over six feet tall and a hockey star. His eyes are this cold clear blue: way below zero. His muscles are as thick as his bones, his shoulders rounded with them. He looks at my paper bag and my egg container.

"What you got for lunch, Lori?"

"Seaweed." I sit sideways in the desk in front of Lill. I stare him in the eye, take out a peanut butter sandwich, and chew slowly, like I'm eating his stubbly face. Stephanie is talking to the egg girls. She sits down in front of me, wiggling to get on the desk, and waits for Darren to walk over. He's been chasing her a few weeks and they're an almost-couple.

Stephanie opens her sour cream container and fluffs the Kleenex around her egg. She tickles its cheek and then pulls a Tupperware container of salad out of her lunch bag. Darren walks over and sits on a corner of her desk.

"What, is it Easter already?"

"This is Bartley. He's my baby." She smiles up at him: play along?

"He's kind of small, isn't he?"

"Looks just like you, Dar!" Rod makes a pumping motion with his fist. "But it's a stupid name for an egg."

"Well I think he's perfect." Stephanie lifts her nose and swivels on her desk to face Lill and Faith. "So, how many children do you want after you get married?"

"Two. Maybe three," says Lill. "What about you, Lori? How many do you want?"

"None."

Everyone gets quiet, like they want me to say more.

"You don't want any?" asks Faith. "Isn't that kind of . . . queer?" She sits up straight and takes a deep breath, trying to hold the corners of her mouth still, eyes darting back and forth to see if she's being appreciated. Stephanie tangles her hands together in her lap and gives Faith a funeral smile. Lill giggles.

"As queer as you, Faith?" I say, and the peanut butter sticks to the roof of my mouth. I've heard this before. Just because I'm big and I'm a jock and I tell people what I think, they whisper that I'm gay. It's not true. At least I think it's not true. Sometimes I'm not sure. My uncle Wallace is gay. Mom can't seem to get over it. She keeps saying that it was because he was different and everyone kept telling him he was gay. He heard it so often, she thinks, he got to believe it. Nobody's going to tell me what to be.

Stephanie looks at me, maybe worried my feelings are hurt. She doesn't see Darren grab her egg container and balance it on his head.

"Whee! Hey, Mommy! Look at little eggy!"

"Give it back! That's my assignment. If you break it, I'll lose marks." Stephanie jumps off the desk and tries to snatch the container off his head. He lifts it arm's length.

"That's pretty difficult stuff," Rod growls. "Girls get to carry around eggs and get marked for it." He nods slyly at me. "Go Darren! Let's see her jump for it!"

He watches Stephanie's breasts bounce when she tries to tug Darren's arm down, and I'm embarrassed for her. I get up.

"Look out!" Rod says. "There's a big defenseman coming for you!"

He leaps up and stands in my way, but I'm fast. I dodge around him and then both Darren and I have our hands on the egg container. I push him into the blackboard and try to wrench it out of his hands.

"Lori, don't. Just let him, okay?" Stephanie says. "It's going to break if you do that."

"Hey, I'm not the one who's doing something wrong." My voice comes in little grunts of breath. Darren tugs once, hard, and my thumbs slip off the stiff lid edge to the soft middle of the container, crunching it together.

"Oh no, Lori," Stephanie whines, as Darren and I let go of each other, and open the nest. Even the yolk is broken, the Kleenex yellow, slimy, and sopping. The blue baby bonnet has Bartley's guts all over it.

"What are you blaming me for?" I say. "I wasn't the one that took it in the first place."

"Oh, I'm sorry, Steph," Darren says, and Stephanie turns away from him, pretending hurt feelings.

"You're such a pig, Darren," she says, but I can see her smiling, her voice flirty. It makes me angry.

"Hey, look what I've got!" Rod is standing by my desk, holding my egg container to his stomach. "Come and get it Lori. I know you want it."

I walk over. Too bad Nick and Mur aren't here. I'd love to wipe that grin off Rod's face. His smile gets bigger as he tightens his grip on the container. The lid pops up and rests loosely on top.

Quick, I knock the lid off with one hand, grab the egg with the other, and sprint out of the room, clawing the door so it slams behind me. I run, the egg like a glass football in my hand. If I can get to the gym stage without them seeing me, I can go to the place Stephanie and I always used to go to talk about guys. I'll be safe.

All the big sports equipment is kept on the stage, and because the equipment room is being remodeled, there are boxes of baseballs and basketballs, dozens of pairs of skis leaning up against the wall, and a mound of volleyball nets next to the high jump pit. I hop over the volleyball posts and make my way to the far end of stage left. Through the curtains come the noon hour screams of grade seven floor hockey. Then, there's another sound: my name being howled out by Rod, Darren, Lill, Faith . . . and Stephanie. I hide behind the vaulting horse and look around the side through a draped badminton net. I watch them push through the curtain and stand on the green stack of tumbling mats. They look right toward me. Stephanie, the traitor, told.

"I want your eggy, Lori," Rod calls, sing-songy and he walks closer. I look around for something to protect myself with. There is an old, soggy volleyball stuck between the wall and the spring-board beside me. I tug it loose, stand, and get Rod in the forehead.

"Bitch."

He's looking around like he doesn't know what to do. I drop down. Another volleyball, hard, hits the top of the vaulting horse. I look around the side. He's got a whole box of them.

"Lori, Come out," Stephanie calls, as the hard white balls slam into the equipment around me, coming closer and closer. Then one hits. I get it off the wall, in the back of the neck. I clench my teeth so tight they almost break, stand up, and catch myself.

"Stupid dyke," he spits, grinning, tossing a ball from one hand to the other. Stephanie won't look at me.

I take aim. The egg hits Stephanie in the mouth.

I walk past them into the gym. I feel as if I've won my first gold at the Olympics, but no one is cheering.

THE MONARCH

My brother Albert was a catcher of butterflies. That's what Mom said to relatives who lived far away from Grassbank and had never seen us. Albert put his trophies in clear plastic cases, the still wings crisp and delicate on cotton fluff like the soft inside of white bread.

Dad says the first week Albert started grade one, I had chased the bus. I remember crying because I wanted to go with him; it wouldn't have mattered where he was going, either. I had already been to the dankest corners of the basement with him, and would have gone with him to jail, or even the dentist. At six, two years older than me, he was already a man of science in my eyes: brown plastic-rimmed glasses, carrying a book bag and an orange lunch kit. I did finally get to go to school with him, but he was always in a different grade anyway.

Life began at four o'clock when we got off the bus. In spring we had an after school routine. First, we checked on the chickens, making sure that Blind-eye, the half mad rooster, and the hens were fed. Then, if Mom and Dad weren't looking, we'd sneak the old hedge clippers out of the shed to cut alfalfa for the rabbits. It was harder to pull it up by hand, but not even Albert, who was already ten, was allowed to touch the clippers. After dumping a nest of alfalfa into the hutch, it was time for the hunt — for cabbage butterflies and swallow tails, and if we were lucky, the monarch. Sometimes we saw only one monarch in a summer.

The best place to go was the unbroken prairie next to the slough. I wanted to catch butterflies too, but Albert would never let me. He told me that it was his net and so it was his job. My job was holding the mayonnaise jar with the hole-punched lid. So instead of butterflies, I gathered flowers as we went, bunching the stems of blue bells and shooting stars in my fist. This made me lag behind, but he would run back to me to lock his fluttering prisoners in my jar: blue and yellow and russet, pattering softly against a sky of glass. He killed them inside the house on the edge of the bathroom sink, after asking Dad for the bottle of high test gas. He'd put a drop of it on their heads and hold their wings until they were still. He'd pin the little dead things to the cotton.

* * *

I gave up flowers one July. I had proudly shown a blushing pink lady's slipper to Dad and after looking it up in his book, he set me sadly on his knee.

"Now Lila, this is very beautiful. It is also very rare. That means that there aren't very many of them." He paused. "So, what happens to flowers when you pick them?"

"I put them in the encyclopedia and when they're flat, I tape them in my book."

"Yes, but what happens to the flower? Lila? It dies. Some flowers are so rare, they shouldn't be picked at all because there might never be any more. You can pick flowers that we have lots of, but not these. Do you understand?"

I nodded. I had disappointed Dad — and I was a flower murderer.

I slipped off his knee and went to my room. In my scrap book, last year's flowers were crumbling and the tape had yellowed. I opened the encyclopedia and shook out yesterday's flowers, gathered them, soft and wilted, and planted them among the irises near the back door. I did not want to be responsible for the death of beautiful things.

That afternoon, Albert handed me the mayonnaise jar. "Come on!" he said, and I followed him to the field.

Suddenly he pointed. There was a monarch, red and black, shining in the sun. He snatched it off the thistle with his net, then pinned the weak and fiery wings with his fingers. He put it into my jar and clapped the lid on top. We ran back to the house because he was afraid it would tear its wings, beating them against the glass. He wanted to kill it while it was still perfect.

I stood beside him at the sink.

"What if it's the last one?" I said. "What if there aren't any more — ever?"

* * *

Before supper, we went to cut alfalfa for the rabbits. It was tall and ripe, ready to be rolled into the huge round bails that looked as if they could tumble off the hill if you pushed them hard enough. The blossoms were a thousand different purples, yellows, and creams, and the air was hot and thick with them.

To me, they were hardly flowers at all; Dad had fields and fields of them: a harvest of them. Albert chose the tuft with the deepest purple flowers. I hacked away at the tough wad of stems with the clippers while he held them still.

Suddenly, he screamed. When I looked up, he was already running from me, crying "My fingers! My fingers!"

What if I had cut them off? I ran after him but I didn't want to know.

His hand was dripping into the bathroom sink and Mom was looking at it. His face was red and furiously wet. He screamed "You cut off my fingers!" and I ran, terrified, up the stairs, through the first door I saw, slamming and locking it. Albert's room. I could hear Mom calling after me. "His fingers are fine. They're just cut. Lila? Come back!"

I stood still, crying. There, on Albert's desk, was his pile of treasure cases. The monarch was on top, wings drying, spread open to the ceiling. I hesitated, wiping my eyes, then pulled the pins out of its wings. I opened the window and blew the monarch out like a flame.

LIVING DANGEROUSLY

Cam was doing his algebra at the back of the restaurant between taking orders. When he looked up, I could tell he was smiling at me, not at Marina, though she'd already claimed him as far as our group was concerned. She said it was because they were the same age, seventeen. She was with us in grade eleven only because she flunked grade nine. Cam would look up and I'd get this feeling at the back of my head, the feeling you get when someone's playing with your hair. Jenny, his sister and my best friend, said he liked me, too.

I took some of the sweat from my Coke bottle and wiped it on the back of my hot neck. Marina said she liked him first and Marina is the kind of person who lights matches and throws them at you, even when she's not mad. Everybody knows my motto is "live dangerously," but that was a little too dangerous for my taste. I hung around with Marina because she liked living dangerously, too, seemed to have more guts and ideas than I had most of the time, and brought out the wildness in me. I took a peek at Cam and sighed. There was just no way. Marina was in a bizarre mood that evening too, so I knew I had to be careful. She was extra vicious to Jenny, who hadn't done anything, and sometimes she just stared off into space or over at Cam.

Even if you'd never talked to Marina, you'd know to be careful of her. Her hair is long and curly black and she plays up the whiteness of her skin with black eyeliner and red, red lipstick. She looks at you with brittle green eyes, and bites the corner of her lip. Guys she's used call her a witch instead of a bitch, maybe because they're scared of her. She likes that.

We were sitting in the best window booth at the Chinese on one of Jenny's days off when she can sit with us and snap her fingers for service from her brother. It was evening, August, and sweltering. My legs stuck to the red vinyl seat, which was worn out by the sliding of too many bums in blue jeans. In the middle of my seat, there was a rip only partly covered with masking tape, and the foam squished out like blubber from a slit whale. Jenny's dad, the owner, doesn't care about fixing things up. Pops spends his extra money on Chinese lanterns, wall hangings and homesickness in general. Otherwise, he's pretty cheap. He won't get new linoleum and it's starting to break in the high traffic areas, like around the bathroom doors, showing the black lino glue underneath. Guess he doesn't figure appearance is very important, because his is the only restaurant in town.

"Bet you anything she's pregnant, Georgie," Marina said, in the middle of some extra vicious, probably completely untrue, gossip. She leaned across the table as if to whisper to me, but talked as loud as before. She didn't care who heard. "She's never disappeared for so long before, and you should have seen her in the clinic today, trying to think I didn't see her behind that

Seventeen magazine. She was bigger — I swear — and white like she was going to have a nervous breakdown."

"You mean you didn't go right up and ask her if she had a full load? That's what I would have done," I said, and Marina eyed me with admiration. I twirled a curl of my blonde, newly permed hair around one finger and smiled at her, not sure whether I was lying. Cruelty bubbled out of my mouth so easily when I was with Marina. My dad was ashamed of me, and I was starting to get ashamed of myself.

"Yeah? You probably would have, you maniac. I would have, but I just didn't think of it." Her eyes narrowed. "Geez, as if her gut hanging out wasn't enough to prove it." She stabbed out her cigarette, sat back, and curled her upper lip into a sneer, as if I'd told her she wasn't trying hard enough to be nasty.

True, you'd notice if Carmen got bigger. She used to look like a dry cornstalk with wispy hair the color of your old cigar-smoking grandma's teeth. When she filled out, it was like overnight. She stopped walking all hunched over since she didn't have a cave for a chest anymore, but then she found that people didn't stop calling her names anyway. The names just changed because she had basketball boobs.

"Well no wonder she's been gone," Jenny said. "Her parents would probably kill her if she was pregnant. I know mine would. And you've told us stories about her parents, Marina. Like that time when she was eight and had been playing boats down at the river with Arney Ratslaff. Didn't you say her dad beat her with a belt even though she hadn't done anything?"

"Hey, Carmen didn't even know she *could* have been doing something wrong. She didn't know sex existed." Marina bit her drinking straw, spreading her red painted lips away from it to keep them beautiful.

"No wonder she keeps trying to run away," Jenny said, her voice slow and sad. She sprinkled some salt on the table and did a drawing in it. Jenny is artistic and quiet. She keeps me from doing a lot of things that are just too wild, which Marina called "being a drag." When Marina wanted me to do something really awful, she usually had to figure out some way of leaving Jenny behind.

"Pregnant," Marina said again, and made like she was going to spit and enjoy it.

To Marina, like most people, getting pregnant is a sin even though she doesn't think sex is. I think that's crazy. It's like saying it's only stupid to play Russian roulette if you get shot, or it's like saying you're a bad person if something bad happens to you. It's all very confusing to me because people say babies are good things, too, so why are you bad if you have one? People's mothers all had at least one kid, so maybe everyone should just shut up about the kids other people have. I'm a strictly logical type person and maybe that's why this weird world confuses me.

Of course, everyone in Grassbank thinks me and Dad are a little strange, too. He's the art teacher at the high school. He wears an earring and he used to be a freaked out hippie in the sixties. At first, I had a really rough time fitting in here with my city clothes and ideas, the strange earrings my mom sends me, and the fact that Dad and I don't go to any church. I was sort of going through a punk phase then, too, and I wore a lot of black, and one side of my hair was longer than the other, not the kind of style that works well in a small town. Hardly anybody here even has holes in their jeans. Everybody except Jenny said I must be a slut. It almost drove me nuts — until I developed what Dad calls my "attitude" and started hanging around with Marina. After that, if people wanted to talk about me, they had to do it very quietly. Probably, they were more scared of Marina than of me.

"When the nurse said Carmen's name," Marina said, "she just sat there like she was thinking about how she couldn't hide from me any more. She dropped the magazine and walked past like she didn't even know me. Can you believe that?"

I couldn't believe it. Carmen was the kind of person who'd sooner hide behind a magazine forever than face Marina. There was the family thing, too. Carmen and Marina were cousins, children of brothers who may have tried to murder each other way back when they were teenagers, and Marina's uncle Stan went to the hospital with his knee shot up by a drunken bullet.

"She's disappeared lots of times before," I said, holding my face straight. I knew I was looking for trouble, but hey, it's in my nature. I felt a little like I did when I'd taken my dad's car to go jumping on the steep dune road out by the river. Play leapfrog with death. Question what Marina believed.

She looked at me as if she wanted to stuff my drinking straw up my nose, but she didn't do anything about it. Marina remembered everything though, every little bit of disloyalty or doubt. It would swim around inside her like a swallowed goldfish until she could think up her revenge. I thought of what she did to Roberta. She dragged me through a whole rainy Tuesday to spy on Roberta, eventually catching her with Leo when she was supposed to be going out with Don. Roberta had begged and begged her not to tell, but the news was everywhere the next day. I knew it was revenge for something, but I didn't know what.

Out of the corner of my eye, I saw Cam get up and come toward us. He stopped right beside me. I combed my fingers through my hair. Jenny told me he liked it.

"So what do you want, Georgie?" He flipped the pages of his note pad with the end of a pencil and looked at me through his round John Lennon spectacles. I was too careful to look

back. I looked down the neck of my Coke bottle at the frayed
scum of foam at the bottom.

"I want fries and gravy," Marina said. I glanced up. She was
smiling like she was waiting for him to look at her, but I could
tell from her eyes that he didn't. I was thrilled and I couldn't
help looking at him. He was beautiful. His eyes were warm,
dark as black coffee, and his face was strong boned with skin
smooth as china. Quickly, I looked away in case Marina saw.

The week before, I had gone to Jenny's to watch videos —
not anything unusual, seeing as how the Chongs live above the
restaurant and I live across the back alley. We lay on the brown
flecked carpet, which smelled of feet and spilled beer, ate taco
chips and talked about guys when "Night Of The Living Dead"
got too boring; we'd seen it three times before. Cam smuggled
us a couple of whipped cream chocolate milkshakes, right past
his dad, and that was something pretty dangerous to do. He put
them under a bag of garbage in a box he was supposed to throw
away, then took them up the back stairs. I held the cold-sweat-
ing metal cup, wishing Jenny would shut up and watch the
movie so I could ignore both and think about Cam. I heard
Jenny slurp up the last foam of her shake, but my straw got
stuck on a cherry. There were six maraschino cherries at the
bottom of my cup. I tipped them into my mouth, one by one.
Jenny never knew.

Cam was still waiting for me to order.

"I don't want anything, thanks," I told him, tasting the last
acid of my Coke, but wanting cherries instead. He flipped his
note pad closed.

"You sure?" he said, and he sounded disappointed. I wanted
to look up into his clear night eyes to thank him for last week's
milkshake, but I didn't dare, and it made me ashamed.

Marina reached out and touched a billow of his sweatshirt.
"So, what are you doing after?"

"After what?"

Cam looked like he was pretending he didn't know what she was getting at, and walked over to turn up the drippy air conditioner above the door. Jenny clamped her mouth closed and looked at me with little laughs in her eyes. She knew exactly how much Cam couldn't stand Marina. On his way back to his homework, Cam turned on the old clover-leaf fan on top of the dented round-cornered ice cream cooler, and the Chinese lanterns that hung from the ceiling started to turn. The shadow of a dragon crossed Marina's face as she watched Cam sit down and turn away. She looked like she'd had just about enough from life — definitely the wrong time to look at her.

"What?"

"Nothing, nothing," I said, and hoped she'd focus on something other than me if she was going to explode.

"Geez," she said under her breath shaking her head as if I was the most stupid person she'd ever met. It reminded me of the way Mom talks about Dad when I go to visit her in Toronto. She left Dad to try to become a famous artist and said Dad didn't have the guts to do the same thing — that's why he became a teacher.

"I'm going to the can." Marina got up. "Well, you coming?"

I got up obediently. My friend Evan says it's weird how girls always have to take someone with them to the bathroom, or else a whole crowd of them go together. Usually it's to talk about guys, but you never knew with Marina, especially when she was in one of her puppy-strangling moods. In bathrooms, Marina always said things that made me uncomfortable, and made me lie to her even more than usual. A year before, in that same bathroom, just about the time I'd started hanging around with her, she told me about the first time she did it with Andy Weins in the back of his dad's station wagon. I lied, and told her about the time I did it with my nonexistent cousin's nonexistent best friend Herbie, just so Marina wouldn't think I was a child.

She grabbed the key from beside the cash register and we went down the back hall, past the sign that said "Our Bathrooms Are For Our Customers Only." She unlocked the door marked with a bleeding jiffy marker "W". I headed for the mirror.

I fluffed my hair and swayed it forward, making some curls cover one eye. Seductive, wild . . . I hoped. Then I noticed the zit on the tip of my nose. Great. I leaned against the sink to get close to the mirror and check out my face. I stayed clear of the right side of the sink where the whole corner and a lot of the enamel had been whacked off. I used to tell Jenny someone had fallen, brained herself, and Pops had turned her into sweet and sour pork. I usually got a slap on the side of the head for that one.

"I think I know who it is," Marina said, after going into the cubicle and blowing her nose. I could hear her pull down her jean shorts, and then I heard pee spray into the toilet.

"Who who is?" I said, sounding like an owl and feeling stupid.

"Who do you think I'm talking about? Remember Carmen's baby? I know who the father is," Marina said through the partition. I heard her zip up her shorts.

"Who, then?" I mumbled, checking to see if my gold eye shadow really did go with my blue eyes, and rubbing a little foundation on my Rudolph the Red-nosed Reindeer zit. "What baby?" I thought. For all we knew, Carmen was just porking up.

"It's Mark Morin's."

Oh shit. So that was it. She was on a man rampage.

Marina came out of the cubicle and for a second, it looked like she was standing behind a storm soaked window, and her face was getting dragged down with the rain. Mark had dumped

Marina months ago, even before he got a job with C.N. and moved to Rosthern. Everybody knew he was too sweet a guy for her, so she was the only one who was surprised. She took it bad — of course, she takes everything bad. She even stayed drunk for a while, but I thought she'd gotten over it.

"The slut, trapping him like that." Her eyes were black as rat holes.

Carmen was dead meat.

"I've got my brother Larry's car in front of the post office. Come on — we don't need Jenny with us," she said, reading my thoughts.

We left the bathroom. Marina tossed the key back inside before slamming the "W" door; anybody who had to go pee really bad was out of luck. When we walked out of the restaurant I felt like I was being pulled along in an evil wind, too weak to go against it. I only had time to shrug my shoulders at Jenny — no time to see if Cam was back in the kitchen, or in the storeroom, or where he was.

I got into the old wrecked Nova. Marina revved the motor, and squealed the car out of the parking spot, tearing the skin off the tires. I rode all the way across town with my feet on the dashboard because of the mousetrap on the floor. The piece of cheese in it was so petrified, I figured the mice would more likely nibble on my bare ankles. Not that I'm afraid of mice, or anything, just rabies. I would have much rather been driving Dad's car as usual, but it was my fault I couldn't. The week before, we'd been cruising in it and Marina dared me to go a hundred down Main. I did it, of course, right past Dad. I almost peed myself, but Marina told me I was the best.

Marina made me get out and come with her to the front door of Carmen's house.

"Aunt Tina!" Marina exclaimed to the frizzy-haired overweight woman who opened the door. "Long time no see.

We were just wondering whether Carmen would like to go out
to Saskatoon and see a movie or something." Marina craned
her neck to see past the woman into the kitchen.

"A movie in Saskatoon? Getting a little late for that,"
Marina's aunt told her as she eyed the sunset. "Besides, Carmen
isn't here." Her voice was stiff, suspicious, daring Marina to
push her further.

"So where is she?" Marina's eyes shimmered deeply like
pools of cold swamp water.

The woman's eyes narrowed with anger. Her hand made a
fist around the doorknob and she shut the door.

"Poor Aunt Tina," Marina said, and smiled.

It didn't take us long to get to Rosthern, speeding, the Nova
rattling over every pot hole. Marina knew exactly where Mark's
house was. I was glad. I didn't really care if we found Carmen
or not, but I wanted to get this over with. After twenty minutes
of sitting in the car with flipped-out Marina, I wanted to go
home, or hide in the ditch, or something.

The house was on Railway Avenue and there was a beat-up
cardboard sign that said "please use back door", so we went
around. We rang the painted-over doorbell and waited. When
the outside light flashed on, we saw the tall-grassed backyard,
islanded with bits of old cars, and the tired, half-weeded
strawberry patch on the edge of the dirt alley.

Carmen opened the door and stepped back when she saw
us. She was wearing shorts and a man's green work shirt, a
darker green square over one of her breasts where the pocket
had been torn off. Her legs were fat-white and pimpled with
mosquito bites. She did look bigger — fatter, anyway. Marina
pushed in and glared back for me to follow. It was better than
standing in the doorway.

The kitchen was small and had just been painted with globby
yellow paint. Turpentine stink hovered under the smell of

garlic, and the leftover dishes on the counter still had a few reddened worms of spaghetti slithering over the edges. Carmen was leaning against the yellow wall and I thought she might stick to it, or walk away with a yellow swipe down to her backside. Nervously, she put one bare foot halfway on top of the other and gave Marina this hunted look, like an animal somewhere between running and attacking.

It always made me a little sick to see Marina turn someone into a quivering mound of jello, even though I sometimes took part, but the feeling I was getting then was stranger. Carmen looked afraid, but she also looked careful. I felt like an invader — like a brainless Viking pirate who hung out making chit-chat with the farmer he'd captured, just before the farmer's wife dinged him over the head with her frying pan. If you're in the mood to pillage, Marina, I thought, do it and let's get out of here. I stood behind Marina with my back against the wall.

"What are you doing here?" Carmen said, her voice quiet, tense. She came out of the entrance way, sliding her feet over the dirty linoleum, and sat behind the table on the edge of a chair. Marina started to wander around the kitchen, opening cupboards. It reminded me of Marina's mom going through her gym bag and purse, right in front of me, looking for something to slap her for — the pill, condoms, whatever. Marina stuck her head in the living room doorway, then walked over to the sink and looked out the window into the black night; there was no more sunset. I saw her reflection before she turned around. She was smiling.

"Mark's not here." Carmen's voice wavered.

Marina wet her lips.

"You're living in sin," she said, upright, like a TV evangelist. Carmen's mouth opened and she twisted a hangnail until the blood started coming. I thought of her with a tiny tiny baby lost somewhere inside her belly. Absently, Marina lit a match.

Just then, the screen door slammed open and Mark came in. Marina burned herself.

"Hey, look. It's a party, and I wasn't invited," he said, giving Marina a second look as if he couldn't believe she was there, then kissing Carmen. He walked over to the counter and let the chain of fish he was carrying slide like raw liver into the sink. Marina watched him open mouthed, obviously still in love with him.

"I caught my limit, and Ted, he only caught four. How do you like that?" Mark stood uncertainly, looking from Marina to Carmen as if he expected a fight. Carmen smiled at him — this open kind of smile that I'd never seen before — and he smiled back, kind of relieved. "I'm going to run a couple of these jacks over to Dad. Won't be long." He took two fish off the chain, put them in a plastic bag, and banged the door shut after him. Everything was quiet. Somehow the air had changed and it was cooler.

"Get out."

The words were soft, and at first, they didn't seem to be coming from Carmen at all — not Carmen the wimp.

"I don't want you in this house when he comes back." Carmen stood up and stepped forward, moving slowly, her thickening body steady as stone.

"We were just at your mom's. Any messages you want me to take back?" Marina said, unaware of her weak, love struck voice, sounding like she was falling into some hole. Her eyes flamed like dying fireflies.

"You'll tell or she'll find out anyway," Carmen said, and her eyes opened as if she'd heard the words from the angel of truth instead of having spoken them herself.

"I'm getting out of here," I said to Marina. When I got to the car, she was right behind me.

"She is pregnant. She is. You saw," Marina said, desperately hating, and wanting me to do the same. She leaned forward in the dark street, and I backed away, afraid she'd touch me, hang on me, like I'm afraid of stepping on earthworms when they swim onto the sidewalk to die in a downpour.

She drove slowly, like she didn't want to get home, like she wanted to keep me in the car forever. I sat with my arms folded, the cool night air coming in the open window and splashing my face.

"He's going to be damn sorry. Wait until she has a couple more brats and gains about fifty pounds. This one probably isn't even his, you know. The fool. Just wait until I tell Rayleen and Lill about this."

Yeah. Right. Just wait until I tell Jenny and everybody else about this — about how Marina was ordered out of her ex-boyfriend's house by Carmen — Carmen the wimp. Ex-wimp.

Marina wanted to keep cruising, maybe catch a party somewhere if we could find one — anything to keep me around — but I made her drop me off at home. She wasn't impressed with me, but I didn't care. I went around to the back door. Over the fence I saw the back of the Chinese. The outside light went on and Cam came out to hoist a green garbage bag into the Loraas Disposal bin. I waited until he'd gone back inside, then crossed the alley. I said hi to Pops as I passed through the kitchen, then spied through one of the portholes of the swinging doors to see what Cam was up to. His head and arms were flopped all over his books and there was no one else in the restaurant. I went in quietly and sat down in front of him.

He looked up, his eyes very sleepy, and he stretched.

"So, what do you want, Georgie?"

"A chocolate whipped cream milkshake. You know. The special."

I was smiling way too much — so much, my cheeks stung.

SCORCH

 osalie called him Scorch because of his red hair. He could hold his breath until his whole face went dead and his freckles stood out like little rusty light bulbs on a glowing white wall. We thought anyone who could do that was cool.

Rosalie had been my best friend ever since she'd moved on to my bus route about a year ago, and she always thought of wild things to do. Her cousin taught her how to belch-talk, and she could say "no" and even a few swear words. Her dad's wreck of a farm was way out by the old Fish Creek battle site, so she was always first on, and last off, the bus.

Me and Rosalie decided that Scorch should become our friend. Scorch got on the bus right after I did, and he sat by himself in the seat ahead of us.

"Hey, Scorch," Rosalie said that morning, "Gotta show ya sumthin."

He turned around and squinted at her. Rosalie always had a "better not completely trust me" sound to her voice, and no one did completely trust her.

She opened her hands. Inside was a little bleached bone, dirty where it was rough on two end knobs. "So what?" I thought, but I didn't say anything. Rosalie was popular at school, or at least, everyone was afraid of her; they said I was lucky to be her best friend.

He looked down at the thing, then looked up at her. So?

"It's from a person. Dad ploughed it up yesterday. There are leg bones and everything."

He pushed himself far from the back of the seat. He was either trying to get away from the bone or from Rosalie. I don't know which.

"Jessie seen it yesterday. Didn't cha?" She grinned at me.

"Yeah," I said. "You should have seen the skull. One of the plough blades punched it in, and when her dad lifted the plough to turn, he looked back, and there was this thing like a ghost staring at him, black holes for eyes, the blade sticking through its mouth, teeth falling out all over the place. Disgusting."

I had always been good at lying.

Scorch looked at me, horrified, and I lost respect for him. It's true that I looked innocent and people could never really tell when I was lying — but what a load of crap I'd just given him! Maybe he would have known better if he'd known me better.

I looked at Rosalie out of the corner of my eye and knew that she'd seen what I had: that Scorch was obviously not as cool as we'd thought. She looked dangerous: she smelled blood.

"You're scared, arn'cha?" she said slyly, knowing that if he protested, if he said he wasn't, she had him. I was starting to get sick of these games. I hoped he'd say "Oh, yeah. I'm scared. I'm *so* scared, just *so* scared," or something like that. She wouldn't be able to pick on him then.

"Am not!" he said, and all the personality drained out of his face; he seemed to know he'd made a mistake, too, and he didn't know how to save himself yet. I couldn't look at him so I looked into my lunch bag to see what Mum had packed me. Sandwiches, carrots, an apple — but no Laura Secord pudding. I *always* got pudding. I felt kind of ripped off.

Rosalie sat back and laughed. She'd let him think it was over for a while, but I knew she'd be on him again at noon, or spreading the word in the back of Social Studies; Mrs. Lehmann, the Sosh teacher, couldn't see the back of the room very well.

Rosalie looked in my lunch bag, too. Usually she didn't bring any lunch of her own, and when she did, it was sliced baloney and mustard on white, stuck in an old bread bag. Sometimes I shared my lunch with her.

"No pudding? Is your mom on a diet kick or is she mad at you or what?"

My brother Jack told Mum that Rosalie bossed me into giving her my pudding every day. It wasn't true. I didn't always do it.

"Who knows what she's doing," I said to Rosalie, and rolled my eyes around: mothers. Rosalie didn't know what a good liar I was, either.

Rick was waiting for me on the sidewalk in front of the school when the bus pulled up, grabbing a smoke with his grade nine buddies. We'd been going out since the Valentines dance, and Rosalie was jealous. I didn't know whether it was because she wanted to go out with him, or because he was taking me away from her.

"Hey, Jessie," he said in his "cool" voice, so his friends could hear. He came up so close our hips touched, and he put his arm around my waist. Rob and Brent smiled at me like they were in on everything Rick and I did. Charles just giggled, but Charles was an idiot.

Rosalie slapped me in the arm with the back of her fingers.

"Remember the bone, Jessie," she said. "We have to make a plan."

I could feel her standing behind me, angry, but I didn't care. Rick was leading me off to the back of the school; there was still fifteen minutes before the first bell. We went on the step behind Industrial Arts. The door had only a tiny slit of a window, so it was hard to see us from the inside.

He kissed me on the lips, then went down to my neck, as usual. About a month ago, Jack told Mum and Dad I was going around with Rick. They were really mad. They said I was too young and told me to cut it out, but that wasn't going to stop me. Rick was fourteen and I was twelve, and I figured that's pretty old enough.

All of a sudden, the door opened, and there stood Rosalie, jeering at me, with about half our class and all of Rick's friends jumping up and down in the back to get a look through the door.

"Look at this!" Rosalie said, "What a funny color your face is, Jessie. It's red, isn't it?"

Rick jerked away from me like I was hot or poisonous or something, and took off, pushing his way through the people at the door. He bumped right into Mr. Andres, the vice principal.

"What's going on?" he said, looking at Rick, then at me standing all alone on the stairs. "Come on, kids. Break it up."

My face felt like it was burning up into my eyes. I looked at the floor when I went inside, surrounded by snickering. I pretended I was looking for something really important on the top shelf of my locker so no one would know I wanted to cry.

Rosalie came up to me.

"Funny color," she said, but I didn't say anything. "Come on. It was only a joke. Anyway. Look." She held out the bone and a couple of what I thought were horse teeth. "Remember, we're gonna get Scorch."

I wanted to choke her. "How could you do that to me?" I slammed the locker.

"Oh, come on. You can't be mad over that. Did you see Rick run? He doesn't like you anyway. It just shows you who your real friends are."

She had that dangerous look in her eye, and it made even me afraid. She knew everything about me, and she could dump it all and make everyone laugh.

In Social Studies, she whispered things to Monique and Lisa. They laughed and sputtered behind their hands and tried to look like they were copying the notes from the black board. I hoped she was talking about Scorch and not me, and I felt like a coward for thinking it. Rosalie passed me the bone and pointed for me to put it on Scorch's desk. I knew it was a test. The bone felt too hot to keep in my hand, so when Mrs. Lehmann's back was turned, I leaned over and dropped it on page 173 of his text book: the Riel Rebellion.

The bone lay there for about a minute, then slowly, his eyes straight ahead, he put it under the heel of his cowboy boot. He stepped down with all his weight, twisting his ankle, and the bone crackled to bits. He was so cool. He didn't even smile, but he glanced over to me and I could see laughing behind his eyes; he was laughing at both of us, and funny, I wanted to laugh, too. I had never seen Rosalie so mad; she couldn't do anything about it during class, and she was shaking . . . just shaking. Maybe even she believed it was a human bone. I never thought she could be that stupid.

Rosalie led the way to the bus after school. I followed, staring at Rick as I walked past the crowd of smokers. His buddies started laughing and poking him in the stomach with their middle fingers. He wouldn't look at me.

On the bus, I sat with Scorch.

LAUGHING BUCK FAGAN

I rang the doorbell after supper. Buck opened the door. There was a whole hot-dog, bun and all, sticking out of his mouth. He always made a special effort to annoy me.

"Uhhhh! Uhhhhhhh!" He took the hot-dog out of his mouth. "Tarnation, Carnation! You're coming with us again?"

My mom, still hung up on the '60s, had named me Carnation Daisy Newton. I was supposed to be her flower child — get that! In spite of having such a stupid name, I like the '60s: wild clothes and great music.

"Of course I'm coming." Every Thursday night Ms. Fagan had a meeting in Saskatoon, so she brought Angie, Buck, and sometimes me, to the mall. Angie and I could *usually* manage to lose Buck during the first half hour. "And I've told you before, geek, if you don't start calling me Carney like the rest of the universe, I'm going to knock your —"

"Women are aliens, women are aliens," Buck chanted, then made this noise like a space ship, whistling and humming at the same time. Little soggy bits of hot-dog bun came snowing out of his mouth and landed on my boots.

Buck Fagan had always looked like a beaver in a wind tunnel: eyes squinting, nose poking forward, teeth beavering out. Unfortunately, he was my best friend Angie's brother. He was in grade 8, a grade below us. All the girls at school thought he was a freak. He was always trying to make someone laugh, and his favorite thing to laugh about was himself — and his teeth. Pretty warped, eh? He always said that he didn't want braces, because once his teeth were fixed, he wouldn't be able to make people laugh as much.

"Get out of my way, geek," I said.

"Hey! You have to be nice to me today. Remember those guys that followed you and Angie around in the mall last time? Well, Mom has named me your guardian angel. We're going to be together a – all night!"

"You're kidding," I said, but at the same time, I could tell it was true. It was just the sort of thing his mom would do. Being stuck all night with Buck was going to be awful. He'd always be trying to embarrass us, and we wouldn't be able to talk in front of him, or even look at guys without him making a big deal about it.

"Just get out of my way, will you?"

He bounced back and I walked in. The Fagan house made me think of oatmeal, even though everything was supposed to be the best and very expensive. Every bit of furniture, every wall and floor was either light brown or tan. The cleaning lady came twice a week to get rid of the tan stuff that had migrated over onto the brown stuff, and vice versa. Actually, I saw more of the cleaning lady than I did of Ms. Fagan. Maybe that was the way it was for Angie and Buck also. Their dad lived in Saskatoon and Ms. Fagan was always off doing some lawyer thing.

Ms. F. came down the stairs.

"Hello Carney. Don't bother to take off your things. It's time to go. Angela? Aren't you finished yet? Carney's here!"

Ms. Oatmeal, I thought. She reminded me of a bowl of cold grey oatmeal in a suit. I always wondered how someone like her could have had a neat kid like Angie, and a total goof like Buck. Maybe her husband had been like Buck and that was why she divorced him. I could certainly understand that.

Angie came leaping down the stairs, the smile squishing her cheeks up, red and round, and her new coat flying out from her shoulders.

"Yay, Carney! I get to buy my Christmas dress today!"

"Angela! You're not going to wear those earrings are you? Where did you get those things? I've never seen them before." They were tiny golden skulls with glass jewel eyes — not at all biker style, but very artistic. Ms. F. crunched her eyebrows together and looked at me.

"They were supposed to be for Christmas," I said, "but Angie saw me buying them, so I gave them to her right away."

Ms. F. let all the air out of her body and scowled deeper. Maybe the oatmeal was going to boil over.

"You want me to take them off?" Angie said. "To put on some others? I'll go up and put on some others. I'll just be a ——"

"We don't have time. I'm already late for the meeting. Oh, if only you'd start out thinking sense, Angela! Honestly! Skulls in your ears!"

We all went to the garage and piled into the car. I watched the garage door slide open. My mom and dad didn't have an automatic one, so it seemed really weird to me when a door opened by itself, like the house had a trained spook or something.

We drove onto the highway. There was a bright orange glow in the gray flannel cloud above the city. Buck squirmed around in the front seat so he could see us and pointed to it.

"Look. The aliens are landing."

Angie gave me this weak smile that seemed to say "Buck's not my fault."

"There are lots of kinds of aliens," Buck jabbered. "I'm an alien, you're an alien ---- but especially, I'm an alien. I'm the leader of all aliens. Bodunk Crillpitz," he said, then let go a loud damp belch.

"Arthur!"

"What?"

"Please."

"What?"

"Stop it."

"Stop what?"

Ms. F. shook her head. Usually all she ever said on these trips was "Arthur . . . please . . . stop it." He always got too loud, or acted like a jerk, or started connecting up all the seat belts like some sort of horse harness. Once he threw one of her books out the window ---- just to see if she'd notice, I guess. She didn't, so he kept his mouth shut. Angie told on him a few minutes later, but they didn't find the book anyway.

"Now remember, you kids have to stick together this time."

"Mom!" Angie whined.

"Angela, that's enough," Ms. F. said in the stern voice that makes Angie give up and makes Buck try harder. Angie didn't move. Buck giggled and held his hands up so we could see him rub them together.

"Fun, fun, fun. We're going to have fun tonight!"

We double parked across from the mall entrance and Ms. F. handed Angie and Buck some money.

"You look for something nice to wear too, Arthur, okay?"

Angie stuffed her money into her purse. Buck kissed his money, and put it in his pocket. We got out of the car.

"Now, remember what I told you. Stay together."

She drove away. Buck grinned, stretching his lips away from his big choppers.

"Now, remember what I told you," he squawked, waggling a finger at me. "Stay together. Don't fall apart."

"Ignore him Carney."

Angie and I walked past him and through the big glass doors. Far down the hallway under the skylight, in the middle of a million people, was a huge Christmas tree. It was covered with red and green lights that looked like radioactive maraschino cherries. When we got closer, we could see the other decorations. There were plastic icicles, stars, and even chocolate coins wrapped up with gold paper and stamped to look like loonies.

"Look! They've decorated the tree with bucks! Buck bucks! Buck likes bucks!"

I ignored him, and he sagged a little. Angie and I headed for Eaton's, for the expensive dress corner. It was fun shopping with Angie, who could actually buy things that cost a lot of money. I sure couldn't do that. It didn't really matter much, because a lot of the expensive stuff is just too boring.

"Oh, Carney! Look at this!"

She held up a two piece evening dress: a gold sequined tube top with a fluffy black taffeta skirt. We'd seen something like it on the TV movie last week.

"Oh, I couldn't wear this, could I?"

Buck swatted the taffeta. "Is that ever stupid."

"Leave it alone!"

"Go try it on anyway, Angie," I said. "Go on. You never know. Betcha you'll love it."

I pushed her toward the change rooms. A plasticky faced sales lady pounced on her and led her through the curtain. When Angie finally came out, she twirled for us. Buck snorted.

"You look like you've been swallowed by a tube worm from Las Vegas. Only not quite enough of you has been swallowed."

"Carney . . . " Angie looked at me, the panic coming into her voice. I wanted to stuff an old sock into Buck's mouth, or tie him up and leave him for the garbage man.

"It shows too much, doesn't it?" she said. "I was afraid of that. I couldn't possibly wear this."

"Angie, what do you care what he thinks anyway? I like it."

"Of *course* Carnation likes it. This is the girl who wore pink and orange to school yesterday."

"Shut up, Buck. What do you care what I wear?"

Angie started to bite her lips.

"Well . . . I don't know, Carney. Maybe I'll try on some others." She pulled a ruffly, high collared dress from the rack and held it against her, looking up with a gloomy smile to see what I thought.

"Sure, it's nice," I said, but I wouldn't have been caught dead in it: too motherish, too officeish, too oatmealish.

She went back behind the curtain with an armload of clothes.

"Hey! Look at me!"

I turned and jumped back. Buck had put another one of those tube tops over his head and was trying to jab me with his gold sequined nose.

"Take that off before someone sees you."

He began to wave his arms and walk around like Frankenstein.

"Help me! I can't see! A giant Las Vegas tube worm is eating my head! AAAAAH!"

"Idiot!"

I pulled the tube top off his head and sequins frisbeed in all directions. He stepped back and knocked over the 50% OFF rack. The dresses fell right into the boot-dirtied aisle and the glowing plastic Santa from the top of the rack clobbered a little boy in the shoulder. He began to bawl, and the sales lady came hammering over to us on spiked heels.

"Stop! What are you doing?"

Buck grabbed my hand and we ran. I thought "Oh, terrific," as we dodged through the mall. I mean, running is the one thing that makes people really want to chase you. We didn't stop until we got to the food court. Buck threw this huge beaver grin at me, as if we were now a crime team. He didn't let go of my hand until I forced him to.

"Don't you think we should go back?" I said. This was the first time I'd talked to Buck as if he had a brain. "After all, Angie's still in the store and the sales lady knows she was with us. It's not fair to just go off and leave her."

Buck looked at me for a while. "Nah," he said finally, looking down at his shoes. "They won't do nothing to her. And they're not going to come after us either. They're too busy. There are too many people around . . . but I'd wait a bit before going back. You never know."

We walked around the food court, trying to decide what to do. I was nervous. It wasn't because I thought we might get grabbed by the store detectives at any moment. It was because Buck wasn't saying anything — not a thing. He wasn't trying to make me want to kill him.

"You want a Coke or something?" he said all of a sudden.

"Nah."

We were walking past the A&W and I wasn't thirsty.

"No, I meant I'd get it for you."

For a second, I imagined how he'd look without the buck teeth, without the joker card always pasted to his forehead, and it scared me. What was he doing? Was he serious?

"No — no thanks."

He nodded quickly and shrugged, as if to say "Doesn't matter to me." When we came near the Chinese Wok kiosk, he put on his old smile.

"Hey. See this?"

He pointed at a dish of some sort of bean sprouts and sauce.

"Is this spaghetti barf?" he asked the clerk, then looked at me, expecting me to laugh.

"Stupid," I said under my breath and walked away. He followed.

"Hey! Wait up!"

"Listen. I don't care what you do, but I'm going to see if Angie's come out of Eaton's. Just stay away from me, okay?"

"No! No. Mom says we have to stay together."

"She's not my mother."

I swerved around a crowd of people and headed back. He was following me. I ducked around a corner, ran, then hid in the book store behind the last shelf, pretending to read a book called *Delmer the Dodo Eats Dirt*. I had told Buck that I was going back toward Eaton's. Well, I wouldn't. I waited a few minutes and headed for Marz Music.

I looked in the bargain bin, humming to myself, and then a CD on the main shelf caught my eye. I picked it up. The picture on it was neon pinks and greens and yellows. It was a collection of love songs from the '60s, all by the original artists — something that Mom would love. The problem was that it was over twenty bucks with tax. I only had seventeen, and it was out of my price range, anyway. I had never spent so much money on a present before, but I was tempted. I wondered whether Angie would lend me five dollars.

"I'll get that for you."

Buck came up beside me and took the CD. He was standing too close to me so I backed up — just fast enough to be impolite.

"What did you say?" I asked.

"I'll buy it for you."

"No, that's okay."

He was looking me right in the eye. Why wasn't he laughing or doing something stupid? After all, he was the leader of all the aliens, right? It felt as if some spook with a really cold hand had just grabbed me by the backbone.

"I don't want it. Put it back."

"Of course you want it. You were holding it for at least five minutes. I want to buy it for you."

He walked up to the cash register and smiled back at me. His teeth stuck out the same way as always, like bleached wood chips, but his smile didn't say "look at me." It said "like me." The cold hand that had me by the backbone slid up to my neck and I got this choking feeling. I paced up to Buck.

"Don't buy it. I don't want it," I said, with teeth jammed together.

"It's too late. It's yours already."

"It – is – not – mine!"

I walked out.

"Carney? Carney? I'm sorry! I'm sorry for whatever it is that I've done. Please don't be mad. Please."

I stopped and turned around. People were moving all around us and it made me dizzy.

"I bought it already, so why can't you take it? Please take it. It doesn't have to mean anything."

"I don't want anything from you."

I started to walk and this time he didn't follow. Somehow, he'd spoiled something, only I didn't know what. I wanted him back the way he'd always been — laughing. I wanted to bug him and ignore him, and call him a geek, but I didn't think I could anymore.

I walked all the way back to the Christmas tree in the middle of the mall. Angie rushed through the crowd and started swatting me with her scarf.

"What happened? Where were you? I thought they were going to make me pay for all that stuff you wrecked."

"Tell you later."

"Where's Buck?"

"Who knows? What did you get?"

She lifted the Eaton's bag slowly and I looked inside. It was the ruffle dress.

"I know you don't like it, but it's all right. It's kind of grown on me."

I noticed she wasn't wearing the earrings I'd given her either.

"What happened to your little skulls?" I said, pointing to her ears.

"Oh. I took them off because they snagged on the dress. They kind of don't go with what I'm wearing, anyway."

Would she ever wear them again? I wondered what her mother would do if, all of a sudden, Angie stopped trying to act the way her mother expected.

We walked around the Christmas tree to Santa's house where all the kids were lining up. Even when I was a kid, I always felt sorry for the people who had to play Santa Claus. After a while, I figured they'd get sick of wearing the costumes, sick of pretending to be something they're not. We came around the corner and there was Santa, available for knee sitting, present asking, and picture taking.

"Ho, ho, ho," he said.

KICKING DOWN

Hey, Susan," I say. "Are you smart?" She don't look up. She never looks you in the face, always at the floor. The whole class is sitting in the hallway, waiting for Mr. Zarecki to come farting down the hall, his pants sagging underneath his belly, to open the science lab. He's late, as usual, so the kids in other classes are in their rooms already, and we're supposed to be dead quiet. So what?

"Geez, Rosalie asked you a question," Lisa says, her top lip sneary. She looks at me, rolls her eyes and mouths "My God!" Lisa and I've hung out together ever since I dumped my ex-best friend Jessie for hanging out with geeks. Lisa is an ass-kisser. She lets me copy her homework whenever I want and lets me use her pencil case for shooting baskets, even though all the junk inside gets broken. It's pitiful. Susan still don't say anything, probably because she knows us, knows it's a trick. She does think she's smart, even cried once — I seen her — when she didn't get a hundred on a math test, the suck. She's all glasses and freckles, her head turned down and away as if she's afraid I'm going to slap her. If I did decide to slap her, she'd go flying too; she's so skinny, she's shaky when she walks.

"That is so rude, so impolite," Lisa says. "She doesn't even answer a simple question. I don't know . . . "

"You smart?" I say again.

"Sure, I guess," Susan says, quiet, with a shrug.

"Did you hear that? Did you hear that?" I yell. "Susan says she is! She said sure!" I nearly bust a gut laughing. Of course she don't know that Lisa and I changed the meaning of the word "smart" just that morning. To us, it now means pregnant.

"Susan says she's pregnant!" Lisa says, biting her smirking lips, and a few people laugh, a few look, and a few ignore it like they're too cool to be bothered. Susan opens one of her books and sticks her nose in it like always. Kicked down. I hate people like that. My brother Rod says that once people get kicked down enough, they forget how to get up again — as if she ever knew how.

"What is that?" I say, not really asking, as I grab the book away from her. She practically falls over while she's sitting, arms out, scrambling to get it back. It's only a dog book. Everybody knows she likes animals more than she likes people. Most of the time when I hear her talking to her friends — she actually has friends — it's about her stupid cat. I look at a few pages of whiny puppies, then go to the front page. It says "To Susan, Love Auntie Julie." It isn't even a library book.

"Give it back," Susan says, but she's not reaching for the book anymore.

"Love Auntie Julie. Love Auntie Julie," I say, as if I'm holding my nose. She looks up and lunges for the book, and I'm not ready. I manage to snatch at a few of the loose, flapping pages, and I hear them rip as I kick her in the ankle. I let go.

"Geez. You thought I was going to keep your stupid doggy book, so you had to go and wreck it. God."

"And she thinks she's so smart," Lisa says, and we both start to laugh again, until I see Mr. Zarecki walking down the hall. Everybody stands up, but nobody goes near him because of the smell. Susan always waits to go in last, hugging her books to her flat chest. I grab Lisa's arm and we wait to see what she'll do, whether we can make her go before us. Probably, she don't want to be stuck all alone in the hall with us, so she darts past, and I come after her, stepping on her heels. She wouldn't make a fist to save her own life.

* * *

It's blizzarding when school gets out, the snow stabbing cold in your face, stinging like bits of glass. I don't go home on the bus because Rod has a hockey game. I figure it's going to be a long, freezing walk to the rink, but Rod stops beside me in his beater. Three of his grade twelve buddies are with him: Darren, who's okay, Henry, who's spaced, and Billy, who's greasy. Rod rolls down the window and the rubber stripping flaps out. The car is falling apart, and Rod, with his new scraggly excuse for a beard, looks the same way.

"You may as well get in," he says, as if he's embarrassed he has a sister. He acts like a jerk sometimes, mostly when he's around his buddies. He gives me lots of rides, though, even drives me to town when it's only me that wants to go, and fixes my bike, because Dad don't do much of anything. Rod is five years older than me, and we even play catch sometimes in the summer. He's the best hockey player on the whole team, and he's got girlfriends, too. He says so, anyway. Billy opens the back door and shoves over so I can get in. I never been so close to him before. Underneath all that dirty hair hanging to his shoulders, he's got practically no neck.

The guys look at me and I look back. So what?

"Hey, Rod, couldn't you find me a girl who's a little older?" Billy says, and winks as if he's a stud. I'm disgusted. Rod moves his head around and shrugs, like he can hardly wait to kick me out of the car once we're at the rink and I'm no longer in danger of my toes turning black and falling off from frost bite.

"Couldn't you find me someone a little smarter?" I say, and everybody laughs, especially Rod. He likes it when I'm a smart-ass.

"Your little sister has a mouth on her," Billy says, leaning back to sneer at me, like he's trying to show everyone a thirteen year old couldn't possibly insult him. He pokes me in the ribs with his elbow, so I jab him back, harder, and his face twitches once, like it hurt.

"Little bitch," he says, and grabs me in the stomach as if he's tickling, but he's not. It hurts. It really hurts.

"Ow! Rod!"

Rod jams on the brakes, and before the car is even stopped, he's half turned around, and has Billy by the collar, jerking him back and forth. Darren, the guy in front, grabs the wheel.

"Nobody touches my sister. Get out of my car, asshole." Rod's voice is quiet, so it's even scarier because of the choking sounds coming from Billy. Rod's temper can be a pretty frightening thing. Dad's even scared of him. I seen him flip out sometimes, when Dad's drunk. Once Dad drove me home from something, and he was so smashed, he couldn't even walk to the house. Rod dragged him away from the truck and threw him up on the porch, screaming "You gonna kill Rosalie, and she's just a little kid."

Billy falls over me, he gets out of the car so fast, and when we get to the rink, Rod throws Billy's filthy bag of hockey equipment out of the trunk, into the snow bank. They walk in, and to the change rooms, and I hang out at the food booth.

Grassbank rink is real cheapo. Nothing but tan linoleum, cement bricks and painted particle board in the warm part. The cold part is old and dark with lights hanging down on cords from the ceiling. The rafters are like brown ribs curving up from the floor, and make me think of being inside a whale after the guts have been ripped out. Some parts are white with bulges of frost, kind of like fat.

I buy barbecue chips and a paper cup of Coke, even though the guy behind the counter is just setting up and he says he's not supposed to be open yet. Just then the door opens and the team from Duck Lake haul in their gear, laughing and talking, no idea they're going to be wiped. Just before the door slams shut behind them, it yanks open again and Blaine and Gordie walk in. They're in grade nine, a year ahead of me, and they're jerks, but they're all right. Especially Blaine. Blaine's in junior band, and I seen him go up to people with his trumpet and blast it in their ears. Don't care if he blasts your ear out, don't care about nothing, and you got to admire that. I don't care about much either.

At first I think they're going to pretend not to notice me, then Blaine says something to Gordie, and they grin and walk over. Blaine pulls off his toque and his black hair stands in static all over his head. His lips are waxy red, cracked, and peeling. He's big for his age, and looks like he could almost play in Rod's league.

"Rosalie, look," he says, and then unzips his bomber jacket almost all the way to the bottom. Held in by his arms and the elastic waist, are a few bottles of beer. Nobody is allowed to take that stuff in here. I open my mouth, but close it again.

"I thought you were going to show me some chest hair," I say, like I'm bored, rolling my eyes around to the ceiling and back. They both look angry that I wasn't impressed. Blaine yanks up his zipper.

"Just don't tell anybody," Gordie snaps, and they ram through the doors going to the stands.

The place starts filling up with parents and hockey groupies. I go out to the stands to get a good seat, and wish maybe I'd acted more impressed with the beer, so I'd have someone to sit with. Dad was supposed to come, but most of the time he gets stuck in the hotel bar by the highway, so I don't really depend on him anymore. Me and Rod got no mom either. Dad won't say why she left us or anything except she's not dead. I pick a spot behind the penalty box, figuring I'll get to talk to Rod sometime during the game. Blaine and Gordie are on the opposite side and their voices are hard, sliding across the ice, ricocheting off the walls. The players come out for warm up, so there's stuff to watch before the game begins.

Face off.

Rod scores almost right away, and the place goes nuts, especially this group of grade eleven girls sitting above me. They begin to chant, "Rod Rod Rod Rod . . . " and I join in until the action starts again. Sometimes it's even too fast to follow, and there's the slap of the puck and the sound of skates digging up the ice, feet kicking the boards, shouts shooting back and forth, up to the ceiling. There's not much skating from one end of the ice to the other, the guys having Duck Lake pretty much trapped in their own end until the Duck coach replaces a few players. They swipe the puck and actually get a shot on our goal. Rod gets it back, though, and whips out into center ice, but a Duck goon checks him hard into the boards in front of me.

"Asshole!" I scream, as he skates away and Rod gets up and goes after him. The girls and me start chanting again. "Come on, Rod! Come on buddy! Come on Rod! Come on bud-deee . . . "

But we're creaming 'em, just like I knew it, and it's five nothing by the beginning of the third period. Then Rod scores again, and I think maybe he's even going to get a hat trick this game, when the same Duck goon just mashes him into the boards on the other side of the rink cracking him once in the head with his fist. The asshole can't find the puck for a second, and Rod gets up and rams his fist into his face mask.

"Kill 'im, Rod! Kill 'im!" I yell, and someone throws a beer bottle at the goon — Blaine, probably. It bangs on his shoulder, then crashes down, skittering glass all over the ice. Rod's helmet flies off - he never does it up — and then the goon lands one right on his mouth. Rod goes down.

"Rod!"

I'm running, sliding on the ice, before I think I'm moving, and the ref screams for me to get off. Everybody's everywhere, and Rod's still down. I get there about the same time as the coach. Rod's got his hand over his mouth, and there's blood everywhere — on his hands, face, uniform, on the ice, spattered over the brown bits of glass. I want to look away because my stomach knots into a fist and it feels like I'm going to puke Coke and chips onto the ice. Nobody knows this — they'd think I'm a wimp — but I can't handle blood. Scared of it. Totally. I even fainted once when I saw my own blood gushing out after cutting my thumb with a bread knife.

"My tooth," Rod says to me, spitting red, and I catch a look at the bloody hole of his mouth. He sweeps at the ice with his hand. I know that if a tooth gets knocked out, you're supposed to find it, and stick it back in the guy's mouth, then a doctor can put it back in the hole and maybe it'll be all right. I get on my knees and start looking though the blood and the glass with my bare hands, not caring about the blood anymore, his or mine.

* * *

"What was that?" Lisa asks. "Like someone threw something at me."

"I didn't see anything," I say. We're walking down the hall after we've finished our lunches. I told her all about the game yesterday, how I had to run and get Dad from the hotel, how the coach drove us all to University Hospital in Saskatoon and they stuck the tooth back in Rod's face and picked the glass out of my hand. We're trying to figure out whether we want to watch the grade elevens play floor hockey in the gym.

"Look! It's a bat!" she yells, and runs screaming down the hallway. I bust a gut laughing, hear a couple of other girls' screams and then I see the bat, flying back toward me, a little black shadow zapping through the air. Blaine and Gordie come running from the front entrance with the broom, old, dirty, and snow soaked, shaped like a comma. They take a swipe at the thing as it flies over, as if it's a badminton birdie. I never seen anything so funny in all my life.

"Hey! Chuck me the broom!" I yell, forgetting my bandages, but they ignore me and pass it back and forth between them.

Finally, the bat sucks itself to the brick wall near the ceiling where not even the broom can reach it. A ton of kids gather around to look at it. It's black and fuzzy like a tarantula, with these little cat ears. It's breathing so fast, it looks as if it's going to have a heart attack. Blaine looks around like he's trying to find something to throw at it, then runs into the nearest class room and drags a chair under the bat. He steps up on it and swings back with the broom, as if he's using a big fly swatter.

Then, I can't believe it, Susan the nothing steps out of the crowd, grabs the straw part of the broom, and yanks it out of his hands. Everybody stands around with their mouths open. I never even knew she was there.

"Hey!" Blaine says, then turns around and sees the weakling that done it. His face gets red, angry. "Give it back, bitch."He jumps off the chair and grabs for the broom, but she keeps it away. She's biting her lips, her eyes wild and frightened.

"You're going to kill it!" she says, louder than I ever heard her say anything.

"So who gives a shit?"

She darts to the wall and kicks the chair away, almost at him. He jumps back. She starts swinging the broom at him like it's a baseball bat, and he just laughs. So do I, because it looks so weird, this little shrimpy girl going to hit a big guy with a broom — guarding a bat. As if. He lunges for the broom, almost gets it, and she looks like a trapped rabbit, like she knows there's no chance. He goes for it again, and there's this animal look on her face. You can even see her teeth. She flips the broom around and uses it like a spear, ramming it into his stomach. All the air belts out of him in a rushing kind of cough, and he stays doubled over, holding his gut. He puts one hand over his mouth and half runs, half staggers into the boy's can, still bent over. Before the door swings closed, you can hear him barfing his guts out.

Susan is still standing there, calm, looking around like she knows what she has to do and knows she can do it, even if she is scared. Nobody goes near her. She looks me in the eye. She's never done that before, and it gives me a shiver. Her eyes are dark blue, same colour as mine, bigger through her glasses. As soon as Blaine gets out, he'll try to kill her.

I look at my bandaged hands and slide back from the crowd. Maybe no one will see me run to get a teacher.

GABRIEL'S CROSSING

Want one, Naomi?"

I look up from my book, *The Lord Of The Rings*. Annette holds out a liqueur filled chocolate, raising her chin and eyebrows at the same time, her mouth open like the little dot at the bottom of a question mark. Kayleen and Dana watch me from behind, fanning sideways in their desks like playing cards, framing her like ladies in waiting to a fourteen year old queen of diamonds. Queen of lunchroom. I want to keep reading but find I can't look back down to my book.

"Oh! Oh, I'd forgotten," Annette says. "You're dieting again, aren't you?" She looks longingly at the chocolate. "Well, it's got my finger prints on it, so I'll just have to eat it myself."

She places the chocolate in her mouth and kisses the smears off her stubby, pearl painted nails while her mouth is still full.

"You never did have a good memory, did you?" I want to say, but my insides feel mushy, gloppy, ugly as oatmeal, and no words come out. *Yes*, I want to eat the chocolate: gooey and thick and sweet. I also want to smear the chocolate on her face — gooey and thick and sweet. But fat girls never get what they want.

Fat runs in my family, and it ran into me. Mom jokes about this. She says all it would have taken is for some cannibal to have roasted one of our ancestors, like Grandma Dowerchuk, over a spit, let her sizzle down a while, and the family tree could have collected enough drippings to keep us running well with fat for a hundred years. I never say things like this to anybody at school — not that there are a lot of people ready to listen. I'm not popular, and you already know why. I've got these big thick glasses, too, which don't help. They make me look smarter than I am, so once I tried going without them. I kept crashing into desks, fire hydrants and boys I didn't like — and I couldn't read at all, and I love to read. I'm into everything: romance, history, westerns and fantasy. Mom says I'm addicted and my brain's going to rot or explode because my nose is never out of a book. Once, she said maybe I'm reading just to avoid life. I don't know. Maybe I just have a different sort of life.

"Little piggy."

The words wake me like a hard handslap on my desk. I look up. Kayleen said it. She's looking at Annette, not me, and my heart starts again. She pokes Annette in the bum with her toe and Annette lifts another chocolate to her mouth.

"I can't help it. I love Grand Marnier." Annette licks her fingers again, looking pleased that all the chocolates belong to her.

"Eat too many and you'll get drunk," Dana says, jealous eyes on the candy. Annette reaches around and hands back the box.

"Well, get drunk with me then."

There's a movement behind me and I hear a faint laugh.

"Oh, please. What are you? Eight years old?"

I recognise Tip Graham's voice before I turn around, even though this is the last place I'd expect to find her. She's the new kid and never hangs around the school at lunch time. When she came last Christmas, everyone whispered about her coming to live with her grandparents because her parents took off in different directions. I turn my head slowly and see her leaning in the doorway. Her bony hips are tilted under her hands so she looks part model and part gunslinger. She's wearing the same faded, pinstriped jeans she always wears, worn white over the knees and hip bones, and a short little kid's jean jacket. Her hair is blonde and skinny down her back. She spikes the bangs straight up and puts on lots of black eye make-up. Her eye lashes look hard enough to break the skin.

"I *know* I'm not going to get drunk from chocolates. Geez," Annette says, as if Tip is the fool. "But if anyone would know about getting drunk, I guess you would."

"And what's that supposed to mean?" Tip shifts her hips and puts her thumbs through her belt straps, under the invisible holster.

"We heard about you at Gabriel's Crossing last week." Annette looks back at Kayleen and Dana, then sits and smirks as if to say "I don't think I need to say anything more to make you shut up."

Gabriel's Crossing is the local fishing place during the day, and the local party place at night. It's just on the other side of the river from Grassbank, across the bridge and down the old dirt road that used to go down to the ferry crossing before the bridge was built. You always hear about wild things going on there, and to most of the girls in my class, people who go there have to be either sluts or druggies. They think Tip is both. She does hang around with the druggies from grade eleven, so it's probably true.

Tip stands and stares Annette down like a stone outlaw with ivory eyes — eyes that can stay open forever, eyes that don't need tears. Annette shifts her weight uncomfortably and looks away, but her eyes narrow and dart back to Tip. She leans back and whispers something to Dana. It's a loud whisper. I hear the words "drunk" and "all the way." I look back at Tip because she must have heard it, too. She lets a breath sputter through her lips in disgust.

"Come on, Naomi. We don't need this."

I freeze. Sure, Tip is my lab partner in science because we were the last people who didn't get chosen, and I'd hung out a couple of times with her downtown, but everyone is watching now. They're thinking, "Will the fat kid go with the druggie kid?" and if I do, I know they'll talk about me even more than they do now. I glance up at Annette and she's staring at me, this "go away, Naomi" look on her face. My chair scrapes the floor horribly when I stand and gather up my lunch and book. I follow Tip out the door.

"Do they have an attitude, or what?" Tip fumes. "Just our luck to get stuck in grade nine, huh?"

"Yeah." I take a deep breath, my heart butterflying because I'm thinking exactly the same thing. Maybe I've found someone who might understand the way things are for me. That hasn't happened since my friend Patty moved away last year. "Yeah, I've got no friends in this grade."

"Good for you. You're not one of the snots."

"Oh, no. I'm an earthling," I say. "Annette is actually from the planet of the snots."

Tip looks sideways at me. "I guess that would explain her green blood and everything . . . You know, you're weird. I like that. Weird is good."

I almost laugh. She understands. She's not the way Annette says all druggies are. She's nice.

She looks at me with slit eyes, as if hoping to detect repressed wickedness. "Are you one of those people who think they always have to go to class?"

"No. Not always . . ." I say, even though I've never skipped out and first class after lunch is English, my favorite.

"Good. I usually take the afternoon off — for good behavior. Let's go."

I get my jacket out of my locker and think about leaving my lunch and book behind. I stuff them into my pockets, just in case. When I turn around, I see Tip watching me, half smiling, almost as if she thinks I'm doing something stupid. Then she smiles wide. Everything's all right. I follow her through the front doors of the school and wonder if I've made a mistake.

* * *

"It's not really a party. It's just a bunch of us kids getting together and renting a couple of videos." I scuff my shoes along the front aisle of the store part of the gas station. Mom only grunts because she's filling a bag with the chips and chocolate bars some old guy just piled in front of her.

I hang out at the gas station a lot after school because no one's home anyway. It's the family business, and it's open from seven in the morning to midnight. Dad's usually lying on the ground with his feet sticking out from under a car, so he's not much company, but I help Mom inside. The best thing about the store is the most impressive selection of junk food in town. We've got boxes of gummy worms, Blue Whales, big plastic canisters of Icy Squares, and every other kind of chocolate stuff you can think of. The junk food is Mom's doing. She loves it even more than I do.

I watch her give the old guy his change and then she sits on the stool in back of the counter.

"Hey, kid. Toss me a pack of O'Ryan's," she says, as the door jingles shut. "Sour cream and onion."

I do and she catches it.

"So where did you say you were going?"

"Joleen's."

"I haven't heard of her before. She in your grade?"

"No. Grade eleven. She's sort of a friend of a friend."

"Okay. You going to be eating at this party?" she says.

"Tip says maybe we'll order a pizza from the Chinese."

"Tip? Boy or girl? This another friend of a friend?"

"Girl. No. We've been hanging out a couple of weeks."

Mom nods and crunches down a chip. It makes me angry, especially now that I'm dieting and I love O'Ryan's chips, too. She doesn't need those calories. Every time I see her, she seems to look bigger behind that counter: fat rolls inner-tubing under her ESSO T-shirt, polyester pants stretched as far as they'll go. It's as if her skin is only attached to her nose, fingers and forehead, and floats everywhere else on a bulgy ocean. I hate myself when I think like this, when all I can see is her fat, but it scares me: that much fat running in the family, running into me.

"So I don't have to get supper for you?" she says. "No snack?"

"No, that's okay."

"You sure? I'm always starving by four o'clock." She gets off the stool and moves toward the coolers, hips wobbling, brushing the shelves. She walks back with what's left of the cream doughnuts Dad bought yesterday, a large chocolate milk, and a plastic wrapped sub. I back away as if she's holding out a gun instead of a sandwich.

"No, Mom. Really, I'm trying to lose a few."

Slowly, the smile slides off her face, as if the skin is greased. She walks past me and puts the food on the counter, then throws this sick and tired look over her shoulder. Whenever she looks like this, I know I'm too much trouble for her.

"Dieting never works, Naomi, especially not with us. You just screw up your system if you starve yourself. I read that again in the paper last week." She slides one hip, then the other onto the stool and shoves her bag of O'Ryan's toward me. "Nobody's going to say I don't feed my kid because I've got to be in this store all day. Eat." Her face is still, round, heavy as water.

I take a chip and chew. The salt shivers my tongue and stings the back corners of my mouth.

Clang. A car drives over the bell hose by the gas pumps. Mom heaves herself around the counter and through the door without looking at me. The chip gets down to my stomach and starts to digest. My mouth wants more. My stomach screams "More!" and I try to ignore it. I sit behind the counter and open *The Lord Of The Rings*. It doesn't work. I close the book and take a handful of chips, stuffing them one by one into my mouth, my brain numb. I watch Mom through the window. She unscrews the gas cap and the fat under her arm waves like a heavy wet towel in the wind. I hate her fat, my fat, the fat that's run into both of us. Maybe it's hopeless. I tear the plastic off the submarine sandwich and bite the soft white bun. It feels so good — eating. Like forgetting.

* * *

I meet Tip outside Joleen's place. She rings the bell and walks in without waiting, as if she lives there and is just saying "Look out! Here I come!" I follow her down the basement stairs.

"So what did you tell your mother?" she says.

"Just that we're watching a video. She didn't ask if Joleen's parents were going to be home or anything else."

"What did I tell you? Home free."

Home free. My stomach sloshes as I go down the last few steps. The people in front of the TV turn and stare as if I'm a housebreaker. They're sitting on a square of pea green shag carpet that looks like it had been picked up at the dump. It goes with the splintery paneling and the uneven cement floor like spinach goes with liver if you hate them both. Unfortunately, pea green is the worst color to see a lot of when you just ate and ate and ate. The chips, the sandwich, the chocolate milk, the doughnuts, bubble inside me. Nerves. Eating was only comforting before the food got to my stomach.

"Hey, everybody. You know Naomi from school." Tip squirms her way between Joleen and Garth, and keeps pushing Garth's knee to make room for me near the coffee table. I sit cross-legged, squashed in, because I don't want to touch Garth or any of these people I've seen but not really talked to. They're all older: mostly grade elevens, with some twelves and tens. Tip and I are the only grade nines. I avoid looking at the two grade elevens who lie necking on the couch.

"Hi," I say to Joleen. She looks past me, nods, and goes back to watching TV. I turn my head to see Tip because I think she can save me from this lonely sitting in a crowd, not talking to anybody. She sits, chin on her knees, hugging her legs. She doesn't look like the kid gunslinger among older kids. She looks more like a half-grown black-eyed raccoon, one the zoo keeper forgot to feed.

There's a siren, then a loud explosion on TV. Cop show. I don't like cop shows much, but I want to know which movie this is. I'd ask Joleen, but she's watching, and my voice would probably crack and sound stupid among the gunshots. I slide back a little so I have more room and can actually move my legs, then slip my book out of my pocket and hide it in my lap. I'll read when I figure nobody's watching.

"Don't call me squirt!" I hear Tip say. I look up. She's talking to Rod, a grade twelve who's grinning and pulling a stringy slice of pizza out of the box on the coffee table.

"Okay — L'il Orphan Annie." Rod goes back to his place on the floor, laughing, and Garth laughs so hard, I think he's going to pee himself.

"O-Orphan Annie! Ho ho!" he explodes.

"What a jerk," Tip whispers to me, her eyes so narrow, the lashes look like a row of needle-legged tar-drowned spiders. She notices my book and looks at me, eyes suddenly wide.

"You brought a book? What are you? Crazy?"

We look at each other for a few seconds, the party swimming around us like the world outside a fish bowl.

"Hey, L'il Orphan Annie! Toss a beer over, huh?" Garth lies down with his hands under his head, careful not to touch me. Tip reaches under the coffee table, and whips the bottle at him. He sees it just in time to pull out his hand and catch it before it hits his head.

"Hey! What are you trying to do? Kill me?" He reaches behind me and gives her a slap on the back of the head.

"Ow! You'll pay for that," she says.

"Who's going to make me?"

"Me. And Naomi." Tip puts her skinny arm around my shoulders and Garth stares at me a while before shaking his head and turning back to the TV. Once he's not watching, Tip takes away her arm.

There's the sound of heavy boots on the stairs, and I look back. Gangling legs walk down, then there's a box and arms with elbows pointed out as sharp as house rafters. His face is pimpled, older. He walks over the cement, dipping his head so he doesn't crack the bare light bulb in the middle of the ceiling, shoves the pizza aside, and puts the box on the coffee table. I remember his face from somewhere . . . the gas station, and I think I've seen him hanging out at the Chinese.

"So much for the main course. I brought dessert." He lifts an un-iced brown cupcake out of the box and everybody begins talking all at once.

"Novak's muffins are the best. I'll get you one," Tip says, but I hold her arm as she tries to stand.

"No. No food. I've already ruined my diet today." The thought of sending something else down to ferment in my stomach makes me want to run to the bathroom.

"Naomi, silly. This isn't really food." She gets up, leans over and snatches a couple of muffins, then sits back down. "Here. Don't drop any crumbs." She pushes a muffin into my hand.

I stare at it, prepared to feel it flame up on my palm.

"It's only hash, Naomi."

Ice breath in my chest. I don't want this.

Tip looks around like she's afraid someone is taking movies. "Will you just do it?" she whispers. "What are you, some sort of pureness freak?" I look at her and I'm going to try to explain, but her eyes are big and the pupils are small, like she sees a rattlesnake behind me, but isn't going to tell me. "Maybe I shouldn't have asked you along. God, you were going to read! What do you think happens at these parties anyway?"

Slowly, I lift the muffin and take a bite. Tip smiles.

"See? It's nothing. You'll like it," she says, and munches down her muffin. "Eat it all."

I force the rest of it down, and my stomach begins to boil again. I swallow and wait.

"What's it supposed to do?"

"Wait for it," she says. I look at all the people who haven't spoken to me, then look at the TV. It's another car chase - shoot

out. I couldn't care less. I watch to the end of the video and
then someone puts in another. There are voices all around me
and a rushing, inside of a seashell sound. Time is stretched. It
seems like forever ago since I moved. I turn, slow, to see Tip,
and it's so hard to turn, to even lift my eyelids. Tip's there, only
the middle of her through the middle of my eyesight. My body
isn't mine, isn't me. I'm just this speck of knowing inside.

"I can't . . . there's something wrong . . . " I say to my body,
to the people outside my body.

" . . . first time. Just relax and don't fight it. Enjoy it," the
voice says, but I want to stop, and I can't get out, out of my
body. There's a lead blanket holding my arms down, holding
my eyes shut. I feel crying-water on my cheeks.

Arms go around me. I don't know whose. I try to twist and
see, but just my mind twists and I think of how people can start
screaming and not be able to stop. I even hear it, the screaming,
and I smell vomit. I think it's me.

* * *

Someone drove me home — Joleen, I think — and I'd even
gone up the stairs alone, without waking Mom and Dad. How
I did that, I don't know. I expected a lecture in the morning, or
at least a note. There was nothing. Mom and Dad had left early
for the garage and my paper bag lunch was in the fridge as usual.
Everything was as usual except me: numb, dirty joked on, left
alone.

I see Tip down the hallway when I come in late for school.
"Tip, I —"
She walks past me to her locker.
"Tip — what's wrong?"
She twists the combination wheel on the lock then stops.

"God, Naomi. You can't even take a body stone. I was so embarrassed . . . " She shakes her head, and her lips are hard, as if she's clenching stone instead of teeth behind them.

I open my mouth, furious, but close it again. I hadn't wanted that muffin.

"You know," she blurts, "if you can't take it, you shouldn't hang around." She taps the lock with one bitten fingernail and looks sideways at me, nostrils flaring, fed up. I'm too much trouble for her. "And you're always carrying one of those fricking books. You carry it when we go for coffee, you read it at parties, you don't talk to people. No wonder you've got no friends."

She bumps my shoulder as she pushes past me. It starts my insides crumbling: my heart . . . dust. I fumble into my locker, throw my lunch and *The Lord Of The Rings* into the bottom, and run after her.

She looks at me with only half an eye when I catch up to her.

"Party tonight at Gabriel's Crossing," she says, her voice flat, expectant.

I nod.

AVE MARIA

That day when I was thirteen I listened from the back of the church, Mom, Carlin and Rebecca beside me. The choirless choir loft shadowed over us like a thick sky of clouds, light seeping in through small round lights. When Tony Lamont sang, I sometimes couldn't trust myself with his face, and watched the black slippery toe of my shoe instead, or closed my eyes so I'd live only in the sound, and so my mother wouldn't know.

I didn't think she'd know about love. She was so sensible, she liked polyester because it washed well. She *did* love music, though — and she was Catholic in spite of the fact Dad wasn't. I was so thankful she was Catholic because the man I loved was Catholic. I thanked God and all the saints I could think of, and even said a few words to Gitchi Manitou, figuring it wouldn't do any harm. Then I prayed "Please God, let Tony love me too."

He was standing between the flaming candles in front of the altar. His voice was gentle against my skin. He was singing here for the first time since he'd left Grassbank and gone away to University. Every little while, I'd look up, trying to think him closer; I couldn't even see the blue of his eyes from so far away. I looked down again so no one would guess what I might be thinking. After the song was over, I kept his voice warm inside me.

"Lucy? Lucy? Aren't you going for communion?"

Mom was standing, poking me in the shoulder so I'd get up or let her through. The whole pew-full of people was standing, and I was daydreaming next to the aisle, blocking the way. Rebecca and Carlin leaned sideways so they could see around Mom's bum and then stuck out their tongues at me. Mom usually sat between me and the brats because we fought all the time.

I pulled my legs up onto the bench, very ladylike, so no one could look up my dress. Everyone started to move past. Carlin thwacked me in the knee with his middle finger, as if I was a marble, and I stuck out my leg to trip him.

"Weenie," he called me when he stumbled. I pulled my leg back to let all the other people pass, pretending I hadn't done anything.

But what was I thinking? I wanted to take communion: Tony was sitting in front. I stood, followed the last person from our pew, and walked in line to take the host.

I let the round styro-foamy wafer melt in my mouth as I walked back, head bowed like the rest, but eyes roaming, looking for him. He was surrounded by a flock of gray sea-gull haired women: his grandmother and great aunts. I hadn't seen him up close for about a year, so my feet stopped working. He was taller, broader, gorgeouser, and had grown a shadowy little mustache. The man behind me in the line-up bumped into me and I decided not to cause a traffic jam. As I got my feet moving again, I stared at Tony's lips and eyes and cheekbones, commanding myself to remember always.'

"Where were you?" Rebecca whispered to me when I squeezed between her and the arm rest. She'd swiped my aisle seat.

"Where did you think I was, stupid? Swinging around from the lights?"

"That's okay. I know where you were. You were looking at Tony Lamont. I saw you." She smiled the way she does when she reminds me she's prettier than I am. It doesn't matter, because I'm older and smarter.

"So what if I was looking?"

"You love him," she said wickedly, as if she were a minor witch, as if she were twisting a bobby pin into my belly button.

My heart crushed inside me and I hoped she'd leave me alone. I never should have told her I loved him two years ago, way back when I was eleven.

"So what if I do?" I threw back at her.

"Lucy loves Tony. Lucy loves Tony." She licked out each word as if it were a piece of candy.

"Shut up, Rebecca."

She pulled on Mom's sleeve.

"Mom, Lucy told me to shut up . . . and Lucy loves Tony Lamont."

I could have bitten her, right there in the church. Mom looked down at me with this weird smile, as if she didn't know whether to laugh or say I had no right to tell anyone to shut up.

"Oh, Lucy. You're too young for that, and besides, Tony must be eighteen or nineteen by now," Mom said.

How could she kick apart my world like that? I *knew* she wouldn't understand, but this was worse. She was laughing at me — and she was always right. I hated the way she looked at me, her lipsticky mouth pushed down to a small cherry, as if she wanted to pat my head and give me a lollipop. Everything I'd thought, felt, hoped, in the last two years was shredding inside me. If she were right, then I was a stupid *little* girl. I was stupid for thinking, for feeling, for dreaming, for loving.

"I'll kill you, Rebecca. I swear I will," I whispered between my teeth and my tears.

"I'm sorry, okay? I'm sorry for what I said, even if it's true." Rebecca clumped her heels down on the floor. "I don't know why you think it's such a big deal."

I had to bend over then, pretending to pray like a fanatic, pinching the tears off my eyelashes whenever I squeezed my eyes shut. After Mass, I ran for the bathroom and locked myself into a cubicle. I stood far to the back, squashed beside the toilet tank, because I was afraid Mom would come looking for me and try to find my shoes under the door.

There's a trick to crying in a large, echoey, public washroom without being heard. It's all in the breathing. Take in the air, and blow it out. Let the tears come when they have to, and don't fight them. Never, ever, sob. In spite of having to do this, washrooms are still the best places for crying, if you absolutely have to, if you're nowhere near home. This is because of all the toilet paper, and the fact that, if you're in a cubicle, people think you absolutely need to be there and they won't bug you; they'll wait for someone else to get out of the can. The best thing of all is, they won't feel sorry for you and make you cry harder, because they just won't know.

I blew my nose. A bunch of old ladies came jabbering in, and from what they were saying, I could tell they were the ones who belonged to Tony. I opened my eyes wide, as if this could help me hear better, and they started to go buggy from all the green tile and fluorescent lights.

"I'd almost forgotten what a voice Nan's boy has," said one old lady.

"I hear he wants to go off somewhere else next year; he wants to take opera, now!" said the second.

"Toronto!" said the third. "I think she and Joe will put up the money. He has a girlfriend, you know, and apparently she plays in a rock-and-roll band. I think they'll do almost anything to get him away from *that*." She spoke with a squeamish kind of horror, as if she'd just smiled in the mirror and seen a slug lodged between her teeth.

Well, that was it. He had a girlfriend. He'd go to Toronto, leave me forever, and I was a stupid jerk and a cry baby. There seemed to be nothing left for me outside the mint green walls and the smell of Bon Ami. I wrapped my tears in toilet paper, and filled the toilet with them, hoping the thing would clog and cause a flood when I flushed. Tony was as good as gone, and it didn't matter anyway because he didn't care. Mom hadn't even come looking for me; maybe she didn't care either. She was probably downstairs, serving up the Charity Social pie, thinking of what an idiot she had for a daughter. I sat on the toilet seat for a long time, too tired of it all to cry.

The washroom was empty and the church was very quiet when I heard Tony sing again. I made sure no one saw me when I came out and sat in the back pew. There was a small, half halo of light on the ceiling, coming from where he practiced in the choir loft. He sang Ave Maria, and for once, I had him all to myself. He sang just to me. I closed my eyes and the rain angel-danced on the roof.

Mom sat beside me.

"It's wonderful," she said, her voice warm, worried. I tried to smile as if the last half hour hadn't happened.

"Your father is fifteen years older than I am," she said, as if telling me some secret I didn't already know. "Grandma and Grandpa thought I was crazy to marry him, especially since he isn't Catholic, but I was stubborn . . . "

She smiled, beautiful.

"You better come before all the pie is gone. Some people are going back for two pieces." She handed me a ticket and squeezed my hand.

"I'll just stay a little while."

Before she left, she stuck a dewy spray of baby's breath in my hair. Her hand had been sticky with pie and I licked my palm, rhubarb and sweet, as Tony Lamont began Ave Maria all over again.

BELONGING TO THE DRAGON

We hang out behind the gym at the breaks. Today, Evan got bored and started drawing on my jeans. Rayleen raised her skinny pencil eyebrows and swung her hips so the fringe on the bottom of her purse drummed quietly against her leg. Carly and Boyd didn't notice because they were holding hands and looking at each other, as usual. Most of the other guys who had any muscle were off playing football against Wakaw, so most of the girls were leaning against the wall, manless for the morning like me. These are the girls who act like having a man is the same thing as having a life. Like, grab a brain. I've generally gone out with whoever . . . whoever wanted me, as long as he wasn't absolutely disgusting. It is nice to have some guy around all the time, but you don't have to act as if you're going to marry him, or anything.

My mom would have compared Evan to James Dean, but my mom compares most guys I know to James Dean. (She likes rebels. Who knows why she married my dad? He's a cop.) Evan's tall and not too thin, and he dresses weird: bizarre T-shirts, ratty leather . . . artistic. He does have the Elvis haircut and the deep, kind of tortured looking eyes, though. Maybe he even has the attitude to go with them. The thing that makes him different, the thing he can really do, is draw. On the front of his binder is a blue ball-point corvette and a big skull and crossbones with doodles and phone numbers floating around between. The back is truly amazing: a rearing horse with these wide feathery wings, thunder bolts blasting out in all directions, and everything blowing in the wind. Just wild. This is all I know about him. He's new and he's in my art class.

He started it all by polka-dotting the toe of my running shoe, trying to make me mad.

"You mental?" I said, and kicked him in the leg — not very hard.

He just laughed and his eyes were wicked and hot and blue. It made me feel strange. I looked around as if I expected to see Steve, my boyfriend, even though I knew he was off playing football.

Rayleen watched me closely like she always did. She'd been saying that she was my best friend ever since Steve gave me the ring and I'd started going with him. I knew that if I ever let go of him, she'd be ready to pounce, along with I don't know how many other girls. It is fun to have someone that everyone else wants, even if you do get a little stressed because you're the jealous type.

Evan made a grab for my leg, and before I could jump back, he'd clamped my foot between his knees.

"Hold still," he said, looking up at me. "I'm gonna make you a drawing."

"Geez, Evan," Rayleen said. "What're you doing — asking her to marry you?" She swung around, wanting everyone to look at us — and her.

"Gimme a ciggy?" she asked Evan, real sweet, and then pulled the Marlboros out of his shirt pocket before he even had the chance to answer.

"Sure, I don't care," he said, never taking his eyes off my face.

He started drawing over top of my inside calf muscle. Boyd and Carly and a few others came closer to watch. Everyone seemed to think what he was doing was pretty interesting, so I didn't want to make a scene in front of them all. I mean, when a guy you hardly know grabs part of your anatomy — I don't care whether it's your boob, or your hand, or your foot, you generally get rid of him, right? Especially when you already have a boyfriend. Everyone thought it was interesting, though, or funny, so I thought, what the heck? These are my favorite jeans, but ball-point probably comes out of denim okay.

I couldn't see what he was drawing. It was too low down, and he was leaning over top. All I could see was his black, shiny hair, the strain in his neck, and the lean muscles of his shoulders. I wondered why he didn't play football.

"These are the perfect jeans for drawing, you know, tight. Can you breathe okay when you wear them?" He looked right up into the sun with his hot blue eyes laughing.

"Yeah. Don't be a dork. Ninety-eight percent cotton, two percent spandex." I lifted up the bottom of my jean jacket and plucked the waistband with my thumb.

"Nice," he said, and smiled real shy.

"What are you drawing?"

"Nothing." He acted so innocent. I could feel the sharp pressure of the pen, like a slow moving fingernail.

Rayleen bent down to have a closer look, but he covered the drawing with his hand, warm.

"It's a secret. You can look, but don't tell her." He slid his hand down to my ankle.

Rayleen looked and shrieked laughter in all directions.

"Come on, everybody! You have to see this!"

Rayleen waved for everyone to come closer. They ducked down or squatted to have a look, and came up giggling or with sly eyes.

"He's branding you, Starla," said Carly.

"Evan is a regular Pic–ass–o." Rayleen picked out each syllable of the artist's name. "Pic–ass–o at sixteen."

Evan nodded to them sarcastically, as if he were a king and they were the peasants. Carly smiled and shook her head at me.

"Steve isn't going to like this, Starla," she sang, and I got nervous.

"Okay, my turn. Let *me* see this thing now." I tried to pull my foot out from between his knees.

"Oh, no, no, no," he said, grabbing my leg and clamping his knees tighter. "I'm the artist and you're the canvas, so you've got to do what I say."

Right. I sighed and looked up at the sky. I'm a good sport.

"Pic-ass-o at sixteen."

"Shut up, Rayleen." I glared at her.

Evan moved closer, pinning my leg nearer his body, and then began another drawing higher up, just above the rip in the knee. He held his hand in the bend of my leg, his arm against the back of my calf as if he needed to steady himself to draw. He didn't need to.

Everyone just kept on watching, and it made me more and more nervous. It was like being alone with Evan, only we were in front of a movie camera, or like being trapped down a well with ten people watching for the fun of it but no one bothering to help. What would they say about me after? What would Steve hear?

Evan drew all the way around my leg. It was too high for him to hide this drawing from me, so I could see the horny, twisted spine of a dragon. I've always loved dragons. They're so wild, and fierce, and they're so free. Everyone knows I've been collecting them for ages. He picked up his red pen and drew flames coming out of its mouth and nostrils. It was the most gorgeous thing, and I leaned down, putting my hands on his shoulders to have a better look. He looked right up into my eyes then, and spreading the tear in the knee apart with his fingers, drew a little red heart right on the skin.

There was a crashing metal sound, the sound of the faulty lock on the gym doors. The doors swung open and a few of the football players came out, all wearing their team jackets: Grass-bank Serpents, with a goofy looking bat-winged snake on the back. Steve tried to give me his jacket once. He kept telling me that the serpent was sort of like a dragon, and I kept telling him that it was a stupid looking snake with bat wings. Everybody's hair was still wet from the showers and whatever it is that guys put on it. They must have just gotten off the bus.

"Didja win? Didja win?" the skinny wimp of a Boyd said, as if he was going to die if he didn't find out right away, or as if he had to prove he was cool by liking football, even if he couldn't play it.

They ignored him. We must have lost again, I thought. Then, I saw Steve.

He had stopped, and was watching me and Evan. His mouth was open, like he was almost ready to explode — or puke.

Evan looked at him, still hugging my leg, then went back to drawing.

"You get away from her," Steve said, so quiet, and I got scared then. He looked as pissed off as when he almost took a swing at the vice principal, and then went out and totaled his dad's car. Maybe he was even madder.

Evan stood up and I backed away, right to the gym wall. Rayleen turned her back on me and started to walk, the purse fringe slapping around on her bum. She stopped near the door, so if Steve left, she could go right after him.

Steve rushed Evan before he was ready, and Steve is a tackle. Evan didn't have much chance; he's muscular, but more like a dancer — an artist. Steve slammed him in the eye, snapping his neck around, and he stumbled down into the gravel. Everywhere, people were yelling "Fight! Fight!" and running up to see who it was and who was winning. It was horrible. Evan tripped Steve and then they were rolling around in the gravel. Steve was pounding him.

"Stop it! Stop!" I went forward to try to do something but Carly tugged me back. A bunch of guys pulled Steve off Evan when they figured there was too much blood.

Evan really looked bad. His eye was starting to swell and he was leaning over, letting the blood from his nose drip onto the stones. It was weird, but it seemed like the most important thing to him was not getting his clothes all bloody. I wanted to help him, you know, but Steve grabbed my elbow and jerked me along beside him. He didn't say anything until we'd gone around the corner of the gym, and no one could hear or see us.

"Just what d'you think you were doing, huh? What was that? What is this guy to you? You been seeing him behind my back?" He kept pulling me, walking fast, heading for his car.

I was shaking. I couldn't talk because I couldn't find a word to call him that wasn't a swear, and he was probably mad enough as it was, without me swearing at him.

"He — he was just goofing around, that's all. I didn't even want to let him, but everyone thought it was funny . . . so I let him. You didn't have to hit him! You didn't!"

I was almost crying, and it made him even madder.

"Yeah? What else you letting him do?"

"Steve, he's just this guy from my art class. I don't even know him!"

"But he knows *you*, doesn't he?" He pointed at my leg. "What's that, then?"

For the first time, I saw the hidden drawing that everyone had been laughing about. It was a blue lacy heart, and in the middle, it said "Evan Loves Starla."

I couldn't breathe for a second and I nearly gave up even trying to explain because I figured he'd never believe me. It looked pretty bad. That guy Evan had a lot of nerve, all right, writing that when he knew I was going out with someone — never mind that this someone could beat him to a pulp. I did feel branded then, like a cow.

Steve made me get into his car, the low-slung Trans Am that we cruised in after school. He got in and started it, squealing the pavement black when he pulled out. He was grim-angry now. He didn't look like he wanted to break anyone's teeth, but like he had forced down all the hate, and was letting it blister inside of him.

"So what did you think I'd given you that ring for, anyway, huh?"

I looked down at the delicate gold band with the tiny diamond looking bigger than it was in its silver faced bed: Sears catalogue, $169.99 plus tax. I checked. I had forgotten I was wearing it.

"The ring means I love you and that you're mine, okay? It means you're mine. I even fought another guy to have you, and I won. That means you're mine, too."

He was just as angry, but the hurt was coming out in his voice, and I could see that his lips were moist where he was biting them. It shocked me to think that he loved me. I was scared for him, and I was scared for me.

"I know, Stevie. I belong to you. I know that. Evan didn't let me see what he was drawing, honest," I said, almost whining, afraid I sounded like I was lying, afraid I would lose him. "I belong to you."

I had spoken quickly, and I could hardly believe what I said. I belonged to him?

Steve seemed to settle down a bit. Maybe he could tell I was scared and that I wasn't fooling. I looked at his crew cut, at his thick, meaty neck, the muscles swelling out from below his ears, from below the single hoop earring that had always looked so strange on him. I looked at his eyes; they disappeared like small, flattened footballs between his heavy, soft lids. Evan's blood was still on his knuckles, and I was almost sick. He smiled a bull-dog smile at me, as if he could make me do whatever he wanted now.

"I'm taking you home. You're gonna change, and I'm gonna burn these." He grabbed my leg over the body of the dragon.

I didn't nod or say anything. Did I belong to him? Did I belong to him like his car, or his dog? Could he really tell me what to do, how to act . . . who I could let draw on my jeans?

He parked in the driveway. Luckily, no one was home. I was missing class.

"Go in and change, then bring me those pants."

I got out, ran into the house, and locked the door. I didn't want him to follow. I needed time to think. Through the window, I saw him lean his arm out of the car and light up a smoke. I went to my room to look for something to wear.

Everything good was in the wash or crumpled up on the floor. I could have worn a skirt, but I hate skirts. I lay on the bed, just hopeless, and hugged Puff, my favorite stuffed dragon that Mom gave me. Steve was out there waiting for me, and I wished he wasn't. I took the ring off for the first time since he'd given it to me. It pinched. It felt like a fresh tattoo, or an ear-tag or a brand — just like the heart that Evan had drawn on my leg. I belonged to Steve because he beat some guy up? Because he gave me a stupid rock? I doubt it. I used to feel safe with him because I thought he was on my side, but I think the only side he'll ever be on is his own. I didn't care anymore whether Rayleen got him or not.

I spit on a Kleenex, rubbed the heart off my knee, and changed into a semi-clean pair of jeans. I looked at the drawings. The dragon swirled wild and twined up above the knee, clawing itself out of an inky ocean. At the bottom, at the end of its tail, was the heart. I took a blue pen from my dresser and scribbled inside it until it looked like . . . Loves Starla. Someday, maybe I'd fill in the blank myself. I tossed the jeans on my laundry pile.

But Steve was still sitting out there. I hated myself for feeling afraid, so I grabbed the ring and went outside.

"Hey, Baby — where're your jeans?"

The whole world seemed real quiet.

"The laundry."

"Well, get them."

I dropped the ring in his lap — just stuck my arm through the car window and dropped it. I was so scared, I didn't see anything but his face.

"I'm sorry, Steve. I can't do this. I just can't."

I started walking — fast.

He was yelling. I could hear the engine and the tires, and my feet in the dry leaves. He drove along beside me and I tried not to hear what he was yelling. He stopped the car, ran up behind me and swung me around to face him, shaking me. His hands were on me. His bloody, bloody hands.

"You love *him*, do ya? Do *ya*?"

He put his devil-red face right in front of mine, and I could feel the spit, like venom, come out of his mouth.

"So you gonna hit me too? Go on! Get it over with! I'll have the cops on you so fast —"

For a second, he couldn't decide what to do, then he pushed me, hard. I almost lost my balance, and I was afraid he was going to keep on doing it, but he turned and ran. I could see the snake on the back of his jacket as he got into the car. He drove over the curb when he took the corner and I thought that if he had to total another car to cool off, well, it was okay by me.

I don't remember much of the walk back to school. I was thinking about finding a way to keep ball-point from coming out of denim in the laundry.

BROTHER DEAR

Grassbank is like a lot of other small towns. We have an IGA grocery, a clinic, a drug store, among other things, and a bus depot at the pool hall. Living here, in the land of sheer boredom, can make a normally sane person want to rip off her clothes and leap to her death from the top of a grain elevator. I say "can" because several hundred people live in Grassbank — and they are not dead, though sometimes you might wonder.

I'm waiting to get out of here. It's April and next year's grade twelve, then it's escape to the University of Alberta like my brothers, like Dad wants. If I do what Dad wants.

I have these dreams of running off to Europe for a couple of years, being a nanny and learning a language or two. My best friend's sister did that. If I get up the nerve to do the same, I'll tell Dad I'll do the university thing when I get back. He'll probably explode anyway.

But when I do go to university, I won't come home some weekend with a screwed up head like Greg. He's coming home today and I'm hanging out, waiting for him. I read in my psychology text that the middle kid is always the weird one. When Greg went away to school, he grew his hair long, and every time I saw it, it was a different color. Sometimes I don't believe Greg is real. It's like, I know he exists . . . but not in my dimension, kind of like the Moonies, or like processed cheese food, which my mother compares to plastic and refuses to allow in the house.

And if I did happen to come home with a screwed up head, I wouldn't go shooting off my mouth in front of Dad. Mistake. Last Thanksgiving, Greg started preaching to us about how materialistic we are, about how much gas we use in the cars, about how Dad didn't really need a new motor home, and about how I buy too many shoes. I can't help it. I have a thing for shoes. After Greg left, Dad claimed to be on the verge of a coronary.

"He's a bloody Communist," Dad muttered.

"Oh, come on, Jack! It's Greenpeace he's joined," Mom laughed. She laughs at Dad a lot. Sometimes it makes him mad, but usually it calms him down and he laughs with her. They met in high school and they've been together ever since.

Mom kissed Dad on the cheek. "Besides, we *didn't* need a new motor home."

"He still has his car and everything, Dad," I said, "so don't worry. I think the free world is still pretty safe." I slapped Dad on the back. He's overweight, so sometimes I think maybe he actually is on the verge of a coronary. I imagined how his face might look if I told him I was going to Europe instead of university: boiled red, jaw hanging open: speechless, but not for long. He'd figure out a lot of things to say to me.

Dad shifted into a lower gear of panic during the Christmas holidays when Greg was home again, even though Greg had sold his car. Greg had also learned to shut up a little. They avoided each other, but the tension was still there.

"I don't like movements — environmental, social, political — I don't care," Dad said after Greg was gone. "Movements of any kind sound like they have something to do with the bowels."

Dad never uses the S-word in front of us, but we always get a lot of talk about coronaries, bowels, the pancreas, and the duod-duode-what-ever-the-heck-it-is. That's what you get when you're the daughter of a guy who inherited a John Deere dealership from his father and was always sorry he hadn't tried to be a doctor. This is why he becomes such a Nazi about all his kids going to university. He's got a point. I aim to be the most filthy rich, the most hilariously funny CBC foreign correspondent that the world has ever seen. I know I have to go to university, but this is also a career in which you need to know a lot of languages. There are other things I want to do.

Brother dear, Greg, shows up at the front door about four o'clock, before Mom and Dad get back from work. He's carrying a green plastic garbage bag, which I assume is filled with laundry since he never brings home his garbage to wash, and his beat up army surplus backpack is hanging from his shoulder. I haven't seen him since Christmas, and I'm still not sure I'm seeing *him* because he's got a little wispy beard on the tip of his chin. He must be going for the Old Testament prophet look, but when he smiles at me, he looks more like a malnutritioned devil. I clamp my lips together, but it doesn't work. I spit all over him when I start laughing.

"What?" He frowns and looks down to check if his fly is open.

"Oh, nothing," I sputter. "Did you know that there's a small furry animal hanging from your chin?"

He looks at me in disgust. "And to think I was almost glad to see you." He drops his stuff in front of the door and heads for the kitchen. I follow him.

"You have no sense of humor," I say, as he gets himself an apple and sits down at the table. I pull a chair close to him and sit on it backwards so I can rest my chin on the back and stare at him, eyes blank and bulgy, teeth bared. He hates it when I do this.

"You've been annoying me since the day you were born," he says, trying not to look at me. Eventually he always has to look at me to see whether I'm still staring.

"Live with it. It's my mission in life." My psychology text also says that the youngest kid is always the brat of the family. I consider myself living proof. "So, you got a girlfriend yet?"

He blushes. "If I did, I wouldn't tell you. You'd broadcast it all over the neighborhood."

"Your nostrils are flaring. You're hiding something."

He hates it when I tell him his nostrils are flaring. It just makes them flare more.

"Greg has a girlfriend! Greg has a girlfriend!"

"Sharlene." He swings his long hair out of his eyes and looks at the ceiling — something that always makes him look like he thinks he's better or more mature than me. He gets up and goes to the door, clumping his heavy hiking boots over the tile.

"So leave — snot!" I call, after he's already through the door and it's swinging behind him. His door slams upstairs and I feel awful. As if he doesn't have enough trouble getting along with Dad. I'd been looking forward to him coming home. I hadn't meant to start a fight, but he's just so bad at taking a joke. Greg and I had never been able to have fun together, not like the fun I'd had with Dennis our older brother. Greg never wanted to play catch, to race, to play board games or cards because he's not into "the competition thing." Dad says he's got no drive, no ambition. He's not stupid, but he doesn't really care about being smart. He's in pre-law at university, but his marks are crap. I think he went into law just because Dennis did and Dad hasn't stopped cheering.

Greg doesn't come out of his room even when Dad comes in and falls over the bag of laundry in the doorway, and starts swearing and complaining about how nobody ever puts anything away in this house. Greg hides up there for over an hour, and at first, I think it's because he's mad at me, but then I'm not so sure. His marks have got to be back by now, so maybe he's avoiding Dad. He used to always hide in his room when he had bad news way back in high school.

Mom walks in the front door and falls over the laundry. I hear this big thump and some giggles even though I'm in the kitchen, where Dad and I are making supper, and then hear her feet running up the stairs. After a few minutes, mom comes into the kitchen with Greg, her arm around his waist as if she had to drag him. "You're thinner. I know it," she says to him, prodding him in the stomach.

"I am not." He squirms and avoids looking into her eyes, but smiles. He looks over at Dad, who is already sitting, guarding his dish like a german shepherd.

"Good to have you home, Greg," dad says happily, but his eyes aren't smiling as much as his lips. He doesn't get up. Bet you it's been a year since Dad and Greg have hugged. "Dennis doing okay?"

"I guess." Greg shrugs. "He's doing some research for one of his profs. Says it could turn into a summer job if he does it right."

Dad sits back and smiles as if when Dennis does good work, it feels as good to him as a big meal in his belly. Greg stops looking at Dad and sits on the edge of the chair next to me, like a scrawny bird about to fall off his perch. One side of his mouth curls down and his nostrils are flaring again.

"Greg has a secret," I croon, then slap my hand over my mouth, just remembering about his marks. Sometimes I have an enormous mouth.

"Leave me alone, Sharlene," he snaps, and the room becomes quiet. Dad says grace and then nobody talks, though Mom looks like she wants to. Greg eats the food around his steak. He eats the peas and the salad and starts to scrape the gravy off the potatoes, but changes his mind and smears the gravy back on.

"So. How'd exams go, Greg?" Dad chews his meat and his eyes flicker up, then down again. Greg doesn't say anything for a few seconds.

"Okay."

"Okay? That's all?" Dad leans forward and looks hard at Greg, maybe trying to figure out what he's thinking. Greg puts down his fork like he's finished and is getting ready to run.

"Aren't you going to eat your meat?" Mom says. She sometimes tries to cool things down by changing the subject. "It's your favorite."

"Um, sorry Mom. I'm sort of a vegetarian now."

"You're a — " Dad puts his coffee cup down very slowly, wearing his calm look, but I can tell the word "vegetarian" threw him because of the way his eyes dart around, like he's trying to focus on something he lost. "I'm more concerned about your economics marks than what sort of food fetish you've taken up. What about it?"

Oh, great. Last term, Greg's average in economics was 38%. On this exam, he'd have had to clear 62%, and Greg isn't much into numbers, or money for that matter. I want to put a wall of shatter-proof glass across the table to protect Greg's feelings. He shifts back in his chair.

"Didn't make it."

"What do you mean? You think you failed?" Dad's words are calm, careful.

"Well . . . I couldn't make it. I didn't get to the exam."

I stare at Greg in horror and admiration, hardly believing he has the nerve to tell Dad something like this. Maybe he figures it's better to get it over with sooner than later. Eventually, Dad would see the statement of grades anyway.

"You couldn't make the exam? What was it to you? Some sort of social event?" Dad's face starts to get red, and I feel like it's time for me to start sliding under the table so I won't get hit by any stray exploding brain cells. "What was so important that you 'couldn't make' the exam?"

Greg takes a deep breath and there's this rock determined look on his face which I've never seen before, which I'm sure Dad has never seen before.

"We were at a protest in Edmonton. We picketed the Legislature."

"So, I'm paying your rent and tuition at the best university in the west so you can fart away your time, huh? Ruin your future? Where's your brains? Maybe they just 'couldn't make it', huh?"

"Some things are more important." Greg's voice is very quiet and gentle now, something he told me he learned in psychology class. It's supposed to pacify people who are screaming at you — except it doesn't seem to be working on Dad.

"And you don't have to pay my rent anymore," Greg says. "I got a job. I'm going tree planting this summer."

"You expect to make enough money for the whole year **and** tuition in four months? I knew your math was bad, but — "

"I'm not going back to school."

Greg puts his napkin on the table very slowly. Whenever he and Dad fight, Greg reminds me of one of those gentle, big-eyed jungle animals, like a sloth or a bush baby. He looks like he'd like to scamper up a tree and live far away above the noise and trouble of the forest floor, only this time he looks a little different, as if he'd dearly love to run, but has decided to stay put even if Dad chews him to bits.

Dad starts to blow. "What the hell are you saying? Not going back to school?" I stir my chocolate milk frantically; whenever I'm really nervous, I have to keep moving. I imagine Dad yelling at me, telling me if I don't go to university right out of high school, I probably never will. The spoon tingles against the inside of the glass, so I stop stirring.

"Jack . . . " Mom warns quietly, looking from Dad to Greg to the cold steak on Greg's plate.

"Well, he's ruining his life! If he'd work at it — if you weren't so damn lazy! What about when winter comes, and you can't plant trees anymore, huh? Thought of that? It's those friends of yours, those ideas they've got you into. It's no better than a cult."

"Excuse me," Greg says through his teeth, gets up and walks out the door. That's it, I think. Nobody's ever going to talk to anybody else in this family again.

Mom puts her elbows on the table and rubs her head as if she'd like to take it off and put it in a bowl of cold water in a sound proof room.

"You can't make him do what you want," she says.

Through the door crack I can see Greg's green jacket go past, and I think I hear the front door close. Mom and Dad are too busy starting a fight of their own to notice. I shove my chair back and go after him.

I see him walking down the block toward Main Street. He's got his pack and his laundry.

"Wait up!"

He stops in front of Johnsons' and stands there, not looking back, while I run up.

"You didn't even say good-bye."

"Sorry. I'm sorry. Is that all my family can ever do? Point out what's wrong with me?" He starts walking faster. I look at my watch. The bus for the city leaves at 7:00, in ten minutes. I stretch my legs to walk beside him.

"He didn't mean it — the cult stuff," I say. "You know Dad's temper." Greg keeps walking, taking long ostrich steps. "Why do you always have to run away?"

"If all you came for was to make me feel worse, you can go home. You're no different from Dad."

"He has a point, you know. You could have at least taken your finals. Now, if you ever want to go back, you've got a bad record. They might not want you back. You'll never get to be anything."

"Be something. Be something. That's all I ever get from Dad — from you now, and I know you don't want to go to university, at least not yet. Dad makes a lot of money. He did what his father wanted him to do and he's not happy. Can't you see that? Well, I'm not playing along with that anymore. Be something . . . Sharlene, you're not what you do. You're who you are."

We walk on and I think about this.

"So you never want to be anything?"

He stops and looks at me, his face tight, like he's two millimeters from screaming.

"Do you think I'm nothing right now? Do you think you're nothing?"

I open my mouth, then close it. I play with the zipper on my jacket and think.

"No . . . no, you're not nothing." If going to university is supposed to make something out of you, what are you before you go? Being in grade eleven is no big deal, but it doesn't feel like nothing. I don't feel like nothing.

"You understand what I'm saying?" He looks at me uncertainly, and looks at his watch.

"Yeah. I think I do."

He smiles. "For the first time in your life."

He starts walking and I follow. My brain feels all twisted, like I've just discovered I've been staring out of the wrong side of my head all my life. Greg suddenly seems a lot older, a lot smarter, than me.

"Don't go on the bus, Greg. Can't you just stay . . . until tomorrow?" We sit down on the old iron bench in front of the pool hall. I can see the bus pulling in from the highway.

"Dad isn't going to understand — ever."

"Well, he's especially not going to understand if you run away. If I were you, I'd go right back there and fight it out." I smack my fist into the palm of my hand.

"But I'm not like you. I'm like me. Maybe if I was like you, Dad would like me better."

Greg's voice is low, disappointed, and I feel terrible, terrible, because what he said is probably true. I'm the youngest, the comedian, and I do have more ambition.

"But I like you the way you are," I say, and for one long sick second, I think I'm lying. Then I think that if Greg was different, he wouldn't be Greg at all. Without Greg, who would I annoy? Who'd freak me out with all his bizarre clothes and ideas? Life wouldn't be as much fun. We smile at each other, and the sun is shining in my eyes.

"You like me the way I am?" He looks down at his hands. "So does Kristen."

"Who?"

"You were right. I do have a girl friend. She tells me I'm just fine the way I am, and a few weeks ago, I started to believe her." He stretches his legs in front of him and grins helplessly at his boots, his cheeks pink.

I take in a huge breath of air and am about to shout "Hey, Grassbank, Greg's got a girlfriend," but I find I can't do it. I don't feel like doing something that will make him hate me. I let the air out. "That's terrific, Greg."

"I'd tell you about her, but . . . " He shrugs and looks up at the Greyhound.

"Well, you'll come back. Right?"

Greg watches the bus driver load his pack and his laundry into the baggage compartment.

"Right?"

"I don't suppose I'll stay away forever."

We hesitate, hug, and he gets on the bus. His shadow walks behind the smoked glass and sits alone on the other side of the bus. I look at the cracks in the sidewalk because I'm jealous. He's off on his life adventure, and I'm still stuck in grade eleven. I guess I'd like to run away, too. Someday I will — to Europe. I wave when the bus drives away. I can't see him, but maybe he can see me.

KELLY NEUDORF LEARNS TO KISS

Leslie stands up on the splintering bench to wave. It's the same bench that has "Brad loves Leslie" and "Kyle loves Leslie" and "Jerry loves Leslie" carved on it. She gets her hair caught in the branches, in the spring leaves that flutter in the dim air like moist paper limes.

"Here he comes, Kelly."

"Where?"

I almost fall off the back of the bench, suddenly straining my body to look down Main Street. I am madly, crazy in love with Johnny Nickel. Maybe I'm wanting the moon. I don't know. Yesterday, I thought he was looking at me when I was at my locker, but I was too afraid to turn my head to see if it was true. All the girls like Johnny, and he seems to like all the girls. He's popular and outgoing and funny and wild, and as different from me as Leslie herself. Whenever I act like I'm wanting the moon, my mother looks at me and says the moon is a cold cold place. I don't care. Tonight, I will try to kiss him, or at least make him kiss me. I've decided this. I've promised myself this. I will try to be more like Leslie. I'm terrified.

"He's in the car, stupid. On the passenger side. The guy in the back is his gorgeous cousin Lynden. I met him last month at a dance in Wakaw and he's *mine*." She slaps the leaves out of her hair, and laughs from deep in her throat, mouth open like a woman in a lipstick ad, flirting with the air.

The car, Alex the Chicken's father's car, swings into the parking spot in front of us, crunching the Pepsi can Leslie had thrown into the street. I don't expect to be seeing Johnny beside Alex the Chicken, but I guess he's got to be driving around with someone since he lost his license last month. Leslie jumps down from the bench and leans into the window and the pounding music to talk. She's leaning on Johnny's window and jealousy pain zags through my body.

Leslie can have any guy she wants and not just because she's built and men growl at her in the street. She's got this smile that sends guys into the sky like bunches of balloons. She's got these pale gray eyes and this long white-blonde hair that hangs heavy down her back. She goes to all the parties and gets to meet so many guys, she says she's *crawling* with them, can you believe it? As if they were caterpillars or something. She says they always leave you in the end, just like most of her girlfriends — except me.

"It's not your looks that are keeping the guys away," she told me, a few minutes before, after I complained about my wiry red hair and rusty eyes, and looked down at the back-catcher bruises and mosquito bites on my skinny legs. "It's your attitude. It's what you do. I know it's not really your fault, your parents being so strict, non-fun and non-everything, but you'll have to ease up and stop being so . . . intellectual." She said the word like it was some sort of disease, but was proud of the fact she could pronounce it. "I can help you, if you like."

If anyone can help me, Leslie can, even though it's usually me that helps Leslie out with things like homework, and with life in general. It's kind of weird that this is true, even though we haven't been friends all that long. I guess we need each other. I didn't realize this until the first time I went over to her place. I knew her dad had taken off a few years ago, but I didn't know her mom was hardly ever around. You could tell by the dead tomato plants in the faded milk cartons on the kitchen window sill. I went there pretty often after that, even though my parents didn't want me to, and I think I've only seen her mom twice. Both times she had to stay in with a sprained ankle. Leslie says I'm the only one who hasn't left her. She says even Kathy Klassen, who was her best friend all last year, just stopped hanging around with her for no reason at all. Once Leslie said she wished I was her mom.

The really amazing part of all this, is that Leslie just keeps on smiling and giggling, and sending guys into the stratosphere. I want to be like her, but maybe I'm trying for the moon again. Even if I end up looking like a moron, I can at least try. Anything would be better than sitting at home for another night when all your friends have dates, and your eighteen year old sister, who has both hips and boobs, also has a promise ring. Anything would be better than being sixteen and not knowing what it's like to kiss anybody, thinking maybe you'll never know because you're too shy and too smart. I'd do anything to be normal and popular and have a boyfriend like everyone else. I'm afraid I'm going to turn out like my great Aunt Angel, whose mouth has been waiting in a little sour pucker since she was sixteen. She even looks this way when she sings in church, like she's trying to keep from spitting a peach pit on the hymn book. Dad said she was always such a sourpuss no man would come within a

mile of her, and sometimes he says I remind him of her when
my temper gets out of hand. Thanks a lot. When he says
something like that, I generally just get nastier.

"So tell me what to do," I said to her a few minutes before
the guys drove up, as I emptied my Pepsi. I meant it. For once
in my life, I was going to stop being afraid and try to be the
person I wanted to be.

"Laugh at their jokes, smile and shut up, and try not to break
any arms when you get one of your sudden temper tantrums.
Stop making them think they've got to go around reciting
Shakespeare like you do," Leslie said, and laughed like she knew
everything in the world.

"But I don't go around reciting Shakespeare — well, except
for the 'Double, double, toil and trouble,' part, but everybody
knows that one."

Leslie looked at me as if I was out of my mind. "Trust me.
That's not going to get you anywhere — unless you're interested
in computer geeks like Alex the Chicken. The man is scary. I
didn't know that such extreme nerdness was possible. I think
Grassbank should quarantine him, just in case it's contagious."

Whenever Leslie says things like this, I shrink a little inside,
because there are a lot of kids in school who think I'm a nerd,
too, and nobody knows this, but there was a time when I had
a crush on Alex the Chicken. He's smart — that's for sure —
and when he calls someone stupid, everyone believes him
because they figure he, more than anyone else, knows the
difference between smart and stupid. He calls people and things
stupid a lot because sometimes his sense of humor can get nasty.
He's an outsider like me, even though he goes to all the parties
and dances. Leslie says the guys tolerate him because he's a kind
of mascot, because he's weird, because he says bizarre things,
because he drives them home after bush parties when they're

too drunk to see the tips of their fingers. Sometimes, when he's not being sarcastic, he actually does nice things for people.

But it's Johnny I want now, and I know that if I can just be a little more like Leslie, I might have a chance. Leslie is still leaning into the car, and I wish she would stop and get time moving again. When she finally straightens up, she whirls around like a dancer, being beautiful for the guys, and her hair circles her like a satin cape.

"Come on. Get in Kelly. Party at the Rosthern Regional Park." She leans closer to me and whispers, "It'll be fine. You said your parents won't be back until tomorrow night, right?" She notices me hesitate and looks at me as if I'm something cute. "Come on, I'll be there for you. I'll be with you until I drop you off at your doorstep. You'll be fine. You'll be with Johnny. Just remember what I told you — and watch."

Johnny. Johnny at the party. I have to go. I have to try. If I don't, I'll hate myself for the rest of my life. The only thing I know about bush parties is what my older brother Chris told me — people throwing up, passing out, making out, and eating bugs on dares. But Leslie will be with me, so I'll be fine . . . and Johnny. I used to repeat his name over and over in my head just to make him more mine. Deep breath. You know what they say: to get something you've never had, you've got to do something you've never done.

Johnny gets out of the car because it's a two-door, so he's got to let us in. He's all tall, and leather jacket and blue jeans, and my head lifts up to his eyes, all the way up to the clouds. Leslie walks around, hair swinging around on her back, to slide into the back seat. She smiles like the sun at him, and when he's not looking anymore, she winks at me and mouths "Go for it." I try to walk, swaying like her, but find I can't. I've got nothing to sway with. I can't help smiling, though, because of Johnny.

"You want the front seat?" Johnny looks at me and I stand still. His eyes are wicked like they always are for girls, blue like circles of smoky sky.

"Sure," I say, dazed. He gets in the back, right beside Leslie, and I want to pound my hands on something. He's in the back seat with *her*, not me. The jealousy gets sharper, like having a sprained heart. I sit in the front, in the bucket seat beside Alex the Chicken, and I know that life's not fair.

Alex isn't a chicken, like a coward or anything, but he looks like a starved chicken — he's nothing in comparison to Johnny. He's got such a big Adam's apple, it looks like there's a knee right in the middle of his neck. I can see him easily because he keeps all the dash lights on, and they light him spookily from underneath so his nostrils and cheekbones glow. He looks over at me and smiles, his mouth this intense orange-red, kind of shiny and oozy-looking, as if his tongue might turn to liquid and start dribbling out. He steps on the gas and I get pressed into the back of my seat. Something rolls into my foot. Orange pop bottle: nerd alcohol.

"I haven't seen you at a bush party before," Alex says, and his computer goof brain looks out from behind his glasses. At first, I get afraid because it seems he can see my fear — like he's reading a computer display on my forehead that's flashing "BABE IN THE WOODS, BABE IN THE WOODS." Sure, let Johnny know what a baby I am. Twit. I check the rearview mirror to see if Johnny is listening, but he's right behind me and all I can see is Leslie snuggled under Lynden what's-his-name's shoulder. The guy looks sort of stunned, like he's just won the lottery. I'm relieved. For sure she doesn't want Johnny, I think, then I'm ashamed because she's my friend and she's going to be with me and help me tonight.

Leslie looks up, sees me in the mirror, and gives Alex the finger. He doesn't see it.

"First bush party? Alexie, where have you been? Obviously not to most of the parties *I've* been to," she says, as if she goes to several a night. "I've never *seen* a party girl like Kelly. She parties *all* the way."

Everyone in the back laughs the way people do when they pretend they're not talking about sex. I feel kind of weird, but I sit there and laugh and smile stupidly like I'm supposed to, then look outside to the night, and back to the mirror again. Leslie flashes her "I'm overwhelmed" look into Lynden's face. Whenever people tease her about being a dumb blonde, she smiles, combs her fingers through her hair and says "It's not natural. I'm just pretending."

The laughter cools off and for a while nobody says anything. I'm glad until I hear kissing noises coming from the back seat. The whole world gets quieter until that's all I can hear and think about, and I know that's all everyone is thinking about. My face goes hot and I lean my cheek on the cold window. Up there in the sky is a black sea and the stars are sparkles on the waves.

"So we don't have to teach you how to party, huh?" Johnny puts his chin on the back of my car seat and draws squiggles on my shoulder with his finger. I can smell his cologne, hear the bristle of his stubble on the upholstery. I stop breathing. He's touching me. I want him to whisper now, something just for me.

"But I don't know. Leslie's just another dumb blonde, so maybe she doesn't know what she's talking about." Johnny throws himself laughing into the back of his seat.

His words shock me like thunder and lightning coming from softly falling snow. For a moment, everything is destroyed. How dare he insult Leslie? Doesn't he know what she's been through? I'm so angry, I can't talk, and then the anger gets mixed up with other feelings, love feelings, and I don't want to do anything. I want to forget he ever said it. I always get furious when someone calls women dumb, but I keep my mouth shut. Once, I practically broke Alex the Chicken's arm for making a stupid woman joke. Everybody but Alex had laughing fits over it and I was totally embarrassed. I look over at Alex and he's staring at me, waiting for me to take Johnny's head off. I look out the window.

"I *know* what I'm talking about," Leslie says in a way that sounds like she doesn't believe it herself. She makes a claw-grab for Johnny's gut, and he gives a yell. In the mirror, I see his arm push her further into Lynden.

"Kelly, you've got to come back here and protect me from this maniac woman," Johnny says, and Leslie dives her hands into his stomach again. They wrestle, Leslie squealing like a baby.

"Yeah, Kelly," she bursts out between squeals, "Come back here in spite of the fact Johnny's being a pig. Stop it! Animal! Why should you be stuck up there in the front with the chauffeur? *Ow*! That *hurt*! Come back and join the party!"

Alex jerks his head at the chauffeur crack and stares at me, but I'm already up and squeezing between the seats, thinking only that Johnny actually wants me with him. I squash down so I don't jam myself into the ceiling and try not to step on anyone's feet. Alex takes a corner fast, vicious, and I lose my balance and almost crush Leslie. I squirm my way between her and Johnny. Johnny puts his arm across my shoulders. His cologne is closer now, and there's beer on his breath. The air makes me drunk.

"Hey, there's always something new to learn about having a good time," Johnny whispers. His voice gives me the shivers.

Gravel snaps against the floor under my feet and I've never heard anything so clear in all my life. I am squeezed between my best friend and the guy I've wanted most of all and I've never been so happy. The headlights tunnel through the trees, between the earth and the night. Alex cranks the wheel and we skid into the Regional Park parking lot. Ahead is the picnic grounds then the poplar bush shielding the golf course. There's only one fire and every little while a shadow crosses it like a dark cloud in front of the sun.

Leslie whispers something to Lynden.

"Please? Give you a hug and kiss," she says in her pouty voice, just loud enough for me to hear.

"Now?" Lynden says, and they giggle. I'm supposed to be copying her, but I freeze. Lynden gets out of the car and pulls Leslie after him.

"Yo, babe. You fallen asleep?" Johnny says, and he shoves the front seat forward to open the door. He looks back and smiles with his eyes before he gets out, then takes my hand. I let him help me out, even though I don't need any help.

He doesn't let go when we start following Leslie and Lynden through the tangle of grass to the bonfire. His voice is like melting chocolate. I walk through the dark as if it were the aisle of a movie theatre that goes on forever.

The shadows stretch away from the fire. Alex walks past us and puts down a case of beer. I barely notice the people from school who say hi and look at me weird because they've never seen me at a party before. Every time I see a Wakaw school jacket, I get hopeful because I think it's Lynden and Leslie will be with him, but it's never him. I've lost Leslie. Suddenly, I feel like I can't handle myself. Johnny's hand feels too hot and tight around mine.

"Just got to go ask Les something," I tell him, and let go of his hand. When I walk past Alex, he opens a beer for me and holds it out at arm's length. I take it. I know it makes me look like I belong, but it doesn't make me feel that way. I walk, looking among the people on the grass for one with blonde hair, shining in the firelight. I smell, then taste the beer, because I feel I have to. It smells like rancid jam sandwiches and tastes worse.

Then I see Leslie and Lynden crossing the crowd with a bottle. They walk past the fire and the light rolls around their bodies and they glow like the stolen light of the moon. She laughs and squirms in his arms. I wave to her because I don't know what to do with Johnny, don't know what to do at this thing that's called a party. She doesn't see me, and I feel stupid. Lynden takes her toward the bush. The fire flashes the bottle amber before they disappear.

I turn alone in a circle. I've lost Johnny, now, not only Leslie. I go back to the fire, the only warm place, but veer away because Alex is there, and I don't want to be with him. Finally, I see Johnny. He sits away from the fire, his back against a tree, his fingers guarding the lips of a beer bottle on the ground. There's a girl in a Wakaw school jacket beside him. "He was mine!" my heart screams, and I stand there watching, unable to keep from torturing myself. Alex takes a long branch out of the fire and scribbles red coal on the black night.

I almost can't believe it when she gets up and waves good-bye with her fingers. This could be my only chance — ever. I walk over and sit beside him, ignoring my shaking hands. I put my bottle down on the grass and it tips, but I'm not sorry; now I won't have to drink it. I slide closer to Johnny. He's quiet, like there's nothing inside him but night.

"Kelly," he says, and I wait for him to talk more. I smile, but he's looking more at his bottle than at me. I can't wait anymore. I move against his body, look almost toward him, and wait for his eyes to meet me halfway. If he doesn't kiss me, I'll die.

His nose traces along my cheek and his lips move over mine. What is that? His tongue? I don't know what I'm feeling. I don't know what to do. I just let him do it. I get this feeling that he's not there. He's slow and slobbery, like he's half asleep and doesn't give a damn. I stop and try to look into his eyes, you know, like you're supposed to when you're kissing, when you're in love . . . but he won't look. I keep searching for his eyes and they keep closing, or they slip around to the side like I'm the wrong side of a magnet.

"Got to go take a piss."

He gets up and I realize I'm lying in the grass and my head is hard against a tree root. I hear him walking into the bush and I sit up, dizzy. I think I should be happy, but I don't know. Maybe nothing is ever the way you expect it. It's cold out. I watch Alex. He's stirring the fire. He's so alone, he reminds me of me, and I want to cry. I get up to find Johnny.

Voices come from the right, deep in the bush. It sounds like Leslie and Lynden, maybe going all the way. I wonder what's wrong with me, that Johnny didn't even try. I turn away and find the path that goes down to the slough. Before I'm halfway through the bush, my foot hits something and I nearly scream. It's a body.

"Johnny?"

I hear a moan-sigh and the body shifts like there's someone inside trying to get out. I smell vomit.

"Are you okay?"

Nothing. He doesn't move or make a sound. I stand there for a while, thinking he's dying. But what do I know?

I turn and run, following the firelight to get out of the bush. Alex is still sitting there, about six empty beer bottles beside him, glowing red like a devil tending his own lonely hell.

"Johnny — he . . . I don't know. Maybe he's passed out, or sick."

Alex stands up. "Show me."

We walk through the bush and I think of not crying and not falling. When we find Johnny, Alex shakes him then drags him out of his vomit.

"He had a lot before we came. He'll be out for a while."

I'm glad I can't see him. I try to think of his eyes, his smile, about all the reasons I liked him, but nothing works. There's this hungry cave inside me where there used to be love. All I can think is what an idiot, him lying there in the grass in his vomit. I start walking back. Alex follows me.

"You want to go home?"

Want to go home with Alex the Chicken? More like *have* to.

"You've been drinking."

"No I haven't. Not really. I have one and then just pretend. I put other people's empties beside me."

"Why?" I ask brutally, my eyes dry, the universe my enemy.

"Well, it's better than throwing up."

Just the sound of his voice makes me angry, and I wish he hadn't answered me at all, or that I hadn't invited him to talk to me.

"It's stupid. Why would you pretend to have as few brain cells as everyone else?"

"Oh, hi," he said, making his voice high, a bad impression of a girl. "My name is Kelly and I'm just as dumb as my friend Leslie. Ooo, I love it when you call me stupid."

I want to hit him, but it's more like I want to hit myself. I change directions and walk faster to get away from him.

"Okay, I'm sorry, already." He's close behind me.

"She's not dumb. She's only pretending."

"She *thinks* she's pretending."

I change direction again, but he stays with me.

"Stop following me around. Leave me alone."

I sit on a picnic table, tired of being chased. He sits on the table, too, but he keeps his distance and shuts up so I can tolerate him. He starts to twitch after a little while, like he wants to say something.

"Listen. I'd appreciate it if you didn't tell anyone that I just pretend out here, okay? I mean there's nowhere else to go around here, nobody else to hang around with."

I think about this.

"Maybe you just think you're pretending."

"I'm sorry for that. I got mad when you took that crack about girls being dumb, like you agreed or something. I never thought you would do that, the way you beat on me after I made that dumb joke last fall."

I don't look at him. "You do it. Everyone does it. Pretends. It must work," I say, but at the same time I think of Johnny lying in the bush in his barf. I think of kissing him, but him not looking at me.

"You're not stupid, so don't pretend to be. You might teach yourself."

"Yeah, right. And you're going to stop pretending to be out here getting drunk?"

He's quiet for a while.

"I don't know. Maybe. I will tonight, anyway." He gets his keys out of his pocket. "Let's go."

"What about Leslie? She'll need a ride, too."

"She never comes back with me. Ah, there's tons of cars around here." He looks up at the stars. "Lynden's catching a ride back with his buddies from Wakaw. They'll probably drop her off."

"But she said she'd be coming back with me. She said she'd stick with me tonight."

"Has she?"

The fire begins to snap and spark and it sends a piece of flaming paper into the sky, just over to where the cold cold moon has risen.

Alex and I go to the car. I get into the front seat and turn on the inside light. I don't want to be in the dark anymore.

There is a small vanity mirror on the sunscreen in front of me.
I look myself in the eye. Alex the Brain thinks I'm smart. You
know, so do I.

TEASING BOYS

H ey, look. Is that Roy over there picking garbage? Roy! Hey!" Gail waves before I can stop her and I feel the beginnings of death by embarrassment.

The guy turns. Oh God. It *is* Roy. He's in his Waskesiu National Park uniform and he's putting potato chip bags, chocolate bar wrappers and bits of tree branches in his plastic garbage bag. A lot of branches came down in the storm last night. We'd seen it coming from Gail's parents' cabin: electric white, the kind of storm that sends people to Oz. The beach is cratered with hailstone hollows and there are a couple of wrecked sand castles farther on, toward the weir. Roy starts to walk over. The sand, full of pine needles and cigarette butts, sticks to my wet feet like filthy sugar. I feel naked in just my bathing suit.

"Hi," Roy says to Gail first. Maybe he figures she's not hostile like me. He's not dumb. He just finished his first year of university. "Hi Sophie."

He shuffles his feet and I glance down at the pale blonde hair on his strong legs. He smiles at me the way he used to when we were going out and it makes me furious. Why does he have to be so sweet and so gorgeous and such an idiot all at the same time? The determination to stay away from him slips from my heart into the sand. I think of stupid things he used to say so I can keep myself angry: cutie-pie, sweet baby, baby doll . . . that idiot. We started going out when I was a cheerleader, just before he made the first line on the football team. At first, I thought he wanted to go out with me for the status — the other first liners were dating cheerleaders at the time — and then I thought he really cared about me. But it never worked. I'd start feeling suffocated, and have to get away.

In the car yesterday, on the way here, Gail kept saying I'd get back together with him like the last two times we broke up. It made me mad. I hate it when people tell me I'm going to do something. I announced I was going to become a nun, or marry Tom, her brother who has Down's Syndrome. I shook hands with Tom while his parents laughed and laughed in the front seat. They've been teasing Tom about being my boyfriend for years.

I don't say hi to Roy. We stand like strangers waiting for a bus.

"Hey, you know what?" Gail snaps her fingers. "We're having a barbecue at the cabin tonight. Why don't you come? You know where our cabin is." She looks at the freckles on her arm as if she has a watch. "*Look* at the time! I've got to go. Mom wants me to make dessert."

She turns and runs. I want to take after her and push her in the water but I know I'll never catch her because my legs are too short.

Roy says, "Sophie — don't go."

I try to keep from looking into his eyes, but I can't help it.

"You still mad at me?" he says.

"Yes."

"I said I was sorry."

"And then you called me your 'sweet little baby.' I am not your sweet little baby. You don't have to think you're better than me just because you're older. Wouldn't you hate it if someone called you a sweet little baby?"

"I'm sorry Sophie. I'm only teasing. You know me. I can't resist pushing people's buttons. And you have to admit you have a temper. It's not all me."

He's looking at me with those bright blue eyes, and he's so tall. Being firm isn't so easy when you're standing alone on the beach with someone you sort of almost loved once.

"I can make you happy. You just have to let me."

Before I know it, he's kissing me. I think of Gail telling me I'd get back together with him. My knees start to go weak and Roy lifts me off the ground. Who cares what Gail says anyway?

"Got to go back to work before my supervisor catches me goofing off." Roy puts me down and looks around.

"You're coming to the barbecue tonight?"

He grins. "You know it."

"See you then." I walk backwards down the beach, watching him all the way. I'm smiling so hard it hurts. I want to run into the water and splash and yell and make everyone think I'm out of my mind. Maybe I am out of my mind — at least, if people who are out of their minds can be positively, insanely happy.

I go back to the cabin tripping over tree roots and things, squirrels screaming at me, and I begin to wonder about myself. I was never going to go out with him again . . . so what happened? Surprise, surprise.

Tom comes out the front door to meet me. He's the sweetest guy. He's twenty-five but his parents say he's about the level of a six year old. His eyes are narrow between puffy lids, his face is round, and his hair is combed down from the middle, making a mushroom around his head. He's holding a vase filled with water and wild flowers: small white dogwood blossoms, prairie lilies, and long magenta rods of fireweed. He hands it to me.

"Hey, these are beautiful. Did you get them all by yourself? I'll bet they're going to make a great centerpiece for the barbecue tonight." I take the vase and go inside without waiting for him to answer, because I mostly don't understand him. His tongue is too big, or something, and only his family know what he's saying all the time. I walk through the cabin remembering yesterday, the hail rumbling on the roof. I had forgotten my purse in the car and Tom went out to get it even though his parents tried to stop him. He had turned after taking my purse from the back seat, making sure I was watching through the window, his body beaten with hail. Quickly, I go out the back door and put the flowers down on the picnic table so they'll be for everybody. Gail sees me and bounces off her lawn chair.

"So what happened? Is he coming? Are you back together?"

"Uh-huh." I smile, the inside of my head tickly, fuzzy. I put on my sweatshirt and kick off my thongs.

"I knew it. I knew it," she says, sounding like she won a bet. "Mom! He's coming! Come here, Sophie. Tell me everything."

"I don't know," I mumble. "We kissed, said we were sorry. You know." The happiness in me starts to scatter. Why *did* I get back together with Roy? I can't remember and I start to feel a little ill. Maybe it never works with boyfriends if you think too hard about it.

Tom comes into the back yard and Mrs. Martens sets him to work tearing lettuce for the salad. She shows and tells him exactly how to do it, then calls him a good boy. He sticks his tongue out at her once her back is turned, then smiles at me, bobbing his head in silent, smirking laughter. She always calls him a good boy and I've never thought it was strange before.

Good boy, ha. The man is twenty-five. He's still looking at me, grinning. When he smiles, he looks like any normal person.

"You're so lucky, Sophie." Gail squirms her sandy feet up on the bench and hugs her knees, folding herself small. She's jealous of me because I've had boyfriends and she hasn't. I'm jealous of her because she's tall and skinny. She doesn't realize how horrible it is to be *cute*, your great aunts pinching your round cheeks and talking about you as if you're a child, as if you're too young to understand the English language.

I hear the back gate shut. I know it's Roy even though I don't turn around.

"Baby," he whispers as he puts his arms around me and hugs my shoulders from behind. "I'm hungry."

"Don't call me 'baby,'" I whisper back through his hair, even though he's breathing in my ear and I'm such a sucker for that.

"Teasing," he says. "Teasing, teasing, teasing." He pulls me over to the barbecue to see what's cooking. Tom is staring at us weird, as if we might be dangerous.

"Hey, Buddy!" Roy says to Tom. Like always, Tom puts his hand out to shake, but Roy doesn't see. Roy makes a gun with his fingers and shoots Tom, "P-CHOO," and then gives me a big wet kiss on the cheek. Tom slams a tomato into the salad bowl and lettuce explodes up and over the table.

"Tom! What are you doing?" Mrs. Martens slaps Tom's hand. "You clean that up right now."

Tom starts hucking the lettuce back into the bowl, and out of the corner of my eye I can see Roy shaking his head, as if he's thinking Tom is a baby. When Tom is done, he crashes down to sulk at the far end of the table. I wonder what his problem is.

"He's being a bad boy," Mrs. Martens says to us as if he can't hear, as if there couldn't be a reason for what he did.

"Okay, everybody, come and sit down. Gail, call your father. Supper's about ready."

Gail hollers into the cabin for her dad. Roy sits beside me and Gail sits opposite, skinny elbows on the table, leaning her smirking face on her hands. Mr. Martens comes out of the cabin.

"Hey, kiddo," he says to Tom, who's still sulking at the end of the table. "That's my seat. Why don't you sit by your girlfriend over there?"

Tom jerks his head up as if he's been hit, gets up and stomps out of the yard. Girlfriend. We'd been telling him this forever. How could we? How could we tell him lies and expect him not to believe them? We watch him head down the street toward the beach and soon can't see him because of all the other cabins. I feel awful. I want to go after him, but I want to forget that I should go after him.

"Tom! Tom? Come back!" Mrs. Martens stands up halfway.

"What happened here?" Mr. Martens sits down on the bench.

"Oh, he spilled the salad, and when I got angry, he started to sulk. He's just acting like a child. Maybe I can catch him before he crosses the highway. If he's upset, he won't watch." Mrs. Martens stumbles around her bench, then jogs out the gate and down the road.

Mr. Martens clears his throat quietly.

"Well. Guess we'd better eat. Nothing we can do."

Roy puts a hamburger in a bun for me and starts putting the fixings on. He knows what I like usually, but I wish he'd let me do it. He probably thinks he's being romantic or something.

"Here, eat up, baby," Roy says, and puts the hamburger in my plate. Baby — again. I take a bite out of the hamburger instead of his arm and come away with a mouth full of raw onions. I'm too polite to gob it back into my plate, so I chew it down, the onion gas going up my nose and making my eyes water.

"Why did you put those onions in there? I nearly gagged," I whisper to him. "You know I hate onions."

"These are a different kind. I thought you should try them."

What is he? My mother, now? I take the lid off my hamburger and pull the onions out of the mess of ketchup, mustard, and relish. I feel awful, getting mad over onions while Tom is out there breaking his heart about me. I start eating. Whenever I'm upset, I eat. I can go through a whole bag of Oreos if I'm not careful.

Mrs. Martens comes through the gate.

"I couldn't do a thing with him." She sits down. "I've never seen him so upset. It's got to be from more than just spilling a little salad."

Whoa. Brilliant thought of the day. I reach for another hamburger and wonder if I should say anything. I don't think they'd believe Tom might have normal, twenty-five year old feelings.

"You're not going to have more, are you?" Roy says, watching me scratch the sesame seeds off another bun. "You really shouldn't."

I squash the bun back onto my plate. If I want to eat myself sick, it's my right. I look at Roy stuffing his face, and slide away from him on the bench. I get up.

"I'm going out there with Tom. Where is he?"

"Oh, but that's sweet of you, Sophie. He's in the gazebo on the beach. Try to bring him back before his food gets cold."

I walk out of the yard. The road gravel grinds into my feet before I remember I'm barefoot, but going back is not something I can do. I cross the hot licorice pavement then go over the sand to the gazebo. Tom is sitting on the far bench. His head is down and sometimes he waves his hands and moves his lips as if he's arguing. I hesitate. The wind has picked up and blows cool off the water.

"You okay?" I say. After a long time, he looks up and puts out his hand. I walk over, shake it, and sit beside him. We watch the waves.

MUSICAL FRIENDS

The worst heat came on the day of the Grassbank Town and Country Fair, the day Dan Cuong and I volunteered to work the food booth together. The flies buzzed up like kicks of black gravel against a tin shed, blue iridescent like Dan's hair reflecting the sky. Dan and I'd been buddies since Easter — just buddies. Rumors had been flying around about us, but I never wanted to be anything more than friends, because, well . . . because.

Dan isn't his real name. I can't pronounce his real name because it's Vietnamese and really weird. He's a refugee. He got in with a foster family in town and started coming to school last fall. Nobody wanted to hang around with him at first because he was different and always had this look on his face — as if he was amazed to be alive. Jay and some of his friends called him "the Chink", and Jillian started rumors that he got his clothes at the Salvation Army. After that, it was pretty hard for any of us to be overly nice to him — except for the nerds, but Jillian always said that nerds would be nice to *anyone*.

As soon as Dan started to speak English so that most everybody could understand him, his true personality came out: class clown. The town crowd still thought he was a nobody, but most of my friends started liking him, and that's when I began to think it was okay to talk to him, even though Jillian didn't like him. One day he stopped at my locker when I was in the middle of my Japan kick (which came between my ancient Egypt kick and my astronomy kick), to look at my poster of Mount Fuji and my crappy copies of Japanese writing. I found out then he was like me; interested in annoying people until they go berserk. A minute after he left, Jillian found a sign that said "I Am From Outer Space" stuck to my back. That meant war — of the most hilarious kind. Over the next few weeks I put peanut shells down his pants, he glued my pencil case to my desk, and we had this supreme vanilla pudding food fight in the Home Ec. room.

A greasy blonde guy came up to the food booth counter just after Dan and I had started our shift. I'd seen him a few minutes before when I'd walked through the midway. He ran the Ferris wheel for LeRoy Brothers Carnival Rides. Dan got up to help him.

"Here. A Sprite and two bill dickles," Dan said, as he tossed the money in the cash box and handed him his junk food. I shut my mouth tight but the laugh came out in a long sputter through my lips.

"Say 'dill pickle chips', not 'bill dickle.'" I slapped him on the back with the fly swatter. Mr. Theissen, the man who ran the food booth for the Fair Association, looked up from filling the ketchup bottles and grinned at me. He reached back and turned up the country heartbreak channel on his radio. Steel guitar stirred through the air and base thumped at your hearts mixing with the merry-go-round music from the midway — tinkling bells, repeating over and over, around and around, sweet as candy apples.

Dan chugged down his Coke. "Shawna, I did say 'dill pickle.'" He smiled big and goofy at me, the way that makes people think he doesn't really know what's going on. The year before, even after his English was good enough, sometimes he'd still say the wrong word in class to drive the teachers crazy. Once, when he was supposed to say "heavy drug user," he said "heavy dog user," and it just about killed everybody.

He tried to see if there was a dead fly hanging on the back of his T-shirt where I'd swatted him, turning once then spinning completely around. He snatched his empty Coke cup and dipped it into the bowl of water that held the ice cream scoops.

"Don't," I commanded, and held up the fly swatter for protection. I wouldn't have minded a good splash of cold water on such a blistering day, but not water with sticky ice cream floaties in it. "There wasn't a fly on you in the first place."

He laughed low and wicked and heaved the water. I jumped out of the way and only got a little down my arm, but I hit my hand on the counter.

"SHSHooot!" I flapped my hands trying to shake the pain out of it. I thought seriously of running to the cooler and shoving my hand into a container of ice cream.

"You okay?" He took my hand in both of his, as if holding an injured butterfly, and looked at it. There was a red line across the back, just below the knuckles. His closeness shocked me and I forgot about the pain. I remembered what my friend Gina said; she didn't think Dan wanted to be just friends with me. I listened to the whirling merry-go-round music and let my hand rest in his for a moment. Then, I panicked.

"I'm okay, I'm okay," I said, scrambling for something to say. "But I'm going to get you back for this." I showed him the soggy, chocolate ice cream gunked sleeve of my shirt. "I'm going to take my time about it, though."

I sat up on the junk food table in the middle of the booth, beside the Cheezies and the O'Henrys, and he sat beside me, laughing. Between the splintery wood awning and the counter, we had a pretty good view of the ball field and the midway because the outside counter runs around three sides of the booth. Mr. Theissen bribes people to volunteer at the booth by bragging about how the place has the best seats near the ball park: shade, a good view, and the Coke machine. Business was slow because the home team, the Grassbank Swifters, was playing, and it had been nothing to nothing even up to the ninth inning. People were stuck to their seats — with fascination and sweat. Dan and I sat on the table, watching the game, swinging our legs.

"What's that?" He pointed to the right of the ball field to the edge of the midway, the usual amazed look on his face.

"It's called a Ferris wheel."

Higher than the trees, it was the biggest one I'd ever seen, painted in red, orange and yellow circus zig-zags, the paint cracked, webbed with rust. People filed into the chairs, the greasy carny guy slammed the safety bar over them, and they were off, up and down, around and around, spinning with the music. If you ride enough, you get dizzy, and you don't even notice the seediness of the whole carnival when you're on the top, coming over the crest like riding a wave. The back of your head is light and tickling and you don't think of coming down to the ground, of the oily smell of the engine, its coughs of blue smoke, its chain saw sound.

"Ferris wheel," Dan said slowly, to get the pronunciation right. "Go with me?"

"Why?"

He was smiling like he wanted to get into a lot of trouble. He pointed to an empty ice cream container. "Take a pail. Splash water on people. Listen to them scre-e-am." He grabbed his cup and emptied the last drops of water on my head.

"Hey! No fair!" I gave him a shove and the box of Cheezies fell on the cement.

"What's going on there?" Mr. Theissen called from the back of the booth, where he was getting the hamburgers ready for the grill. "I can see the headlines now: "Food Booth Destroyed In Lovers' Quarrel.""

Dan and I looked at each other. I was about to say "Yeah, right, he's not my boyfriend," when he touched my hand. There was this look of "maybe?" in his eyes. He swallowed and quickly looked down at his knees. I couldn't move. He picked up the pencil from the cash box and wrote "friends forever" on the bottom of the Coke cup.

"Hey! We want some service!"

Jillian. My heart turned to cold water and ran into my stomach. I jumped off the table, away from Dan.

Jillian and I had been best friends since grade three; our farms had been within running distance. She stuck with me even in grade six, when the town girls decided I had germs and refused to touch my desk or my coat, as if I'd smeared all my belongings with earthworm guts. "Who needs them?" Jillian had told me.

"Hi Jill," I said shyly, hoping she'd smile at me, but knowing she wouldn't, not with Jay beside her. She was swinging her arm, maybe trying to make sure I saw her hand in his. She was wearing a neon green bathing suit and a pair of jean shorts. People always called her "Snow White" because of her delicate face, black hair and white skin. She hated the name and said it didn't suit her. That's why she wanted a tan. Mostly, she just got burned.

"Working for free?" she said, and smiled for only a heartbeat before looking at Jay. I wanted to run.

"Two Cokes and a bag of salt'n'vinegar," Jay ordered. He stood in the shade of the awning, his face still, as if he wanted us to know he was bored beyond belief. It hadn't been that long ago when Jay wouldn't say anything to Jillian except call her "pig farmer." I call him "the guy with the fly eyes" whenever he wears his sunglasses, and some of my friends think the name suits even when he's not wearing them. He was holding Jillian's hand, turning his head, watching a red haired girl walk toward the midway and get lost in the crowd. He thinks no one notices what he's doing if they can't see his eyes move. He hasn't figured out that sunglasses make *him* see less, not the rest of us see less.

"God . . . look at that." Jay pointed to the Ferris wheel. It spun like a bicycle wheel off the ground, smooth and easy, as if the music was turning it. "That's Ken up there at the top, and look who he's with! Marette Littlechild. Never thought he was the type that went for squaws."

Jillian laughed and laughed and I wanted to laugh too, to show her we still thought the same things were funny. But it wasn't funny. Marette is my friend.

"What is 'squaws'?" Dan walked up to the counter and put down the drinks and chips. Didn't he know that Jay and Jillian *despised* him? Didn't he know how these things worked? I wanted him to disappear, or change into someone else —

someone with better clothes, someone who didn't have an accent, someone with neatly clipped blonde hair.

Jay looked as if he couldn't believe anyone could be that naive. "What is squaws," he said over and over, under his breath. He looked back at the Ferris wheel. "Ken doesn't even care who sees him."

The wheel was turning, and Ken and Marette were at the bottom, then the top, then the bottom. Dan says none of us are in the same place as we were a second ago because the world turns also.

"Oh, but Jay, it's so romantic," Jillian teased, rolling her big, Snow White eyes at him. She stepped closer to him and squeezed his arm against her body. He hardly noticed. Just then, the people in the stands started to cheer. The home team. A home run.

"Here." Jay threw his money on the counter and turned to leave, pulling his arm away from Jillian.

"I'll be coming right away," she called after him anxiously. "Have to go to the washroom."

But she didn't go. She stood awkwardly with her tongue to her teeth. She curled her finger for me to come closer.

"I can't believe he's wearing jeans," she whispered, and darted her eyes toward Dan. Her smile was like thick paint on a shell. "Doesn't he realize what the temperature is?"

I watched her go. I felt as bad as I did the day she first stopped hanging around with me.

It had been one of those days after I'd forgotten to clean my locker. I opened the door and got a lungful of dirty old gym clothes and drying orange peel. Dan was behind me, gabbing about something I don't remember. Jillian crashed her locker shut beside mine and leaned her shoulder against it, staring me in the face. What was her problem?

"Come on, Shawna. You know how crowded computer class is. We'll never get good seats if you don't come *now*."

She looked at Dan as if he was the slimy thing she'd just dissected in science, then tried to close my locker. She'd been getting weird in the past few months. It had started with her moving to town with her mom, then her dad never coming to see them. Around Christmas, she started to hang around with the town crowd, whether they wanted her or not — like she was getting too good for us farm kids, and Marette, and the others from the reserve. She was also chasing around after Jay and she seemed to think she was getting somewhere. Everyone knew how desperate she was to have a boyfriend.

"Shawna!" Jillian's hands were twitching and her small face was red.

"Okay, okay. Hold on one more second."

She slammed my locker almost before I got my fingers out, then started pulling me down the hallway.

"You're getting more bossy than usual," I joked, but her face was grim. She was concentrating on the door to the computer room near the end of the hallway. When we got there, she stopped, angrily stuck her bottom jaw to the side, and pulled me past.

"What's going on? I thought you wanted to get to class in some big hurry."

She pulled me through the big double doors at the end of the hallway until we were splashing our feet in a shallow lake of snow water. The wind was cold. She turned on me.

"I knew this would happen! Courtney and Natalie got the seats beside Jay. But what do you care?"

"Hey, how was I supposed to know — "

"You *had* to be standing around talking to that dork — maybe telling him how much you love him." She stood back and looked at me as if I was covered with worms.

"He's not a dork!" I shouted, flustered, unable to think of anything to fling back. I wanted to kick water all over her, but stopped myself. "It's not as if you couldn't have walked to class without me!"

"Guess I could have," she said. "You don't seem to know who your real friends are, do you?" She stomped back inside.

When I got to the classroom, Jillian was sitting beside Courtney, just on the edge of the town crowd. The only empty desk was beside Dan, right in the middle of the nerds. At first, I was mad. I thought maybe it was better to be a nerd than a jerk anyway, but all the air around me seemed empty. By the end of the day, I realized she wasn't going to get over it. I felt as if she'd taken out my heart with a spoon.

Splat. Cold water slapped on my runners. I jerked out of my memory. Dan had plunked an ice cream pail of water on the counter between the napkins and the mustard and a wave had slopped out.

"For later, when we get off work." He dropped the Coke cup into the water. "You looked like you were sleeping standing up." He wiggled his eyebrows and elbowed me in the ribs.

"Don't do that!" I pulled back as if his elbow had been the hot greasy hamburger fork. He raised his eyebrows and pushed the hair out of his eyes so he could see me better.

"What?"

"Just don't touch me!"

Mr. Theissen's head jerked up as if I'd just shouted "murder." I guess I had been shouting. I walked away and started wiping the pop drips off the counter, chanting "stay away, stay away" inside my head. Why couldn't he try to be more like everyone else? And why was he wearing jeans? Didn't he know what temperature it was? I looked up at him only once. He looked shabby in his old clothes and grown-out haircut.

He looked amazed and hurt. The crowd in the stands cheered. The Grassbank Swifters had won.

* * *

The supper rush was over about six-thirty. I was afraid Dan would try to talk to me, so I hung around next to the grill, close to Mr. Theissen. Dan wandered around the edges of the booth, cleaning things that had already been cleaned. Every time he looked at me, I felt it. I wanted eight o'clock to come so the shift would be over and I could get away.

"Shawna."

Jillian's whisper. I turned and saw a sliver of her through the barely opened back door. She pushed the door open a little and put her finger to her lips. I waited until no one was looking, then slipped through the door, forgetting my duties. She was standing beside the garbage cans, the flies buzzing sleepy and swollen around her.

"Shawna, you have to come. Now."

"What is it?"

"Can't talk. Not here. Please." Her eyes begged. They looked bruised on the inside. I followed her, feeling the brown porcupine grass crunch like glass under my shoes. We went to the far edge of the fair ground, beyond the ball park, and sat under the trees.

"He — he said it was over . . . in front of everyone." Her mouth opened. She breathed as if she couldn't get enough air. "I thought he loved me. He said he did."

We sat there for I don't know how long. She flung her tears into the grass with her fingers. "After, everybody acted like they'd been expecting it," she said quietly, "like he told them first. They acted as if they didn't even know me."

Musical friends. The town crowd still played that game sometimes. Natalie was kicked out for a couple of months last year. The music stopped and they pulled the chair out from under her. Now it was Jillian's turn to have nowhere to sit down.

"At least I have you," she said, and held on to my hand. She looked into the air and told me everything that had happened since April. My head was whirling with words, and May, June and July blurred together. Everything would be all right. I squeezed her hand.

"Shawna, you have to come with me. Ask your mom if you can stay overnight. I need to talk to you. We've been best friends forever."

But that wasn't right. I didn't want to think it, but I couldn't help it. We hadn't been best friends forever . . . not since Easter. I looked back toward the midway. The Ferris wheel turned slowly in front of the low sun, through the weakened sugar water music. I looked at my watch. Was Dan riding, hating me?

"What are you looking at?" Jillian's voice ran along like fear. She grabbed my arm and made me look at her. "It wasn't my fault. I feel awful about what happened, but it wasn't my fault. I tried to get you into the crowd, but Courtney still talks about you as if we were back in grade six. I'll stick with you this time, though. I'll never do it again."

She turned away from the sun and her eyes were in shadow, looking like dark glasses, or like her face, her whole self, had begun to cave in. There was something so horribly wrong with who she was — who she'd become.

"It doesn't feel good, does it, to have your friends disappear. You're right. You're not going to do it to me again."

"Shawna?"

I stood up. With each word, I had become light: a floating balloon. "We haven't been friends forever. We haven't been friends since April. I didn't do anything to deserve that."

"But that wasn't my fault."

"You're wrong. Or you're lying."

I walked out under the branches. The sun was turning the sky to lime over the midway, and the leaves were burnt green against it. The whole land was darkening, cooling, as if under water, and I felt I was moving so slow. I ran all the way through the midway, past the nickel and dime gambling casino, the cotton candy stand, the shooting gallery, running through the carnival music, swimming in the air. I stopped at the base of the Ferris wheel. Dan wasn't there. The carny guy rammed the safety bar over the person in the last seat. The wheel started to move against the clear sunless sky.

Rain? Two cool drops on my forehead. A few people laughed and clapped and some pointed to the top of the Ferris wheel.

"Dan!"

I saw him turn, silhouetted, find me under the floodlight. He hesitated, waved, and threw a cup of water into the sky.

THE SUN PUSHING THE WIND

Sarah walked out of the house, through the garden, and onto the street that ended in a field. The sun was hot yellow butter on her hair, flowing down neck and arms, the back of bare legs.

She'd only been in Tuxford for a week, but her whole past already seemed to have been a dream, her life having changed into something unrecognizable: treeless fields in four directions, Saskatchewan's dust bowl. It was a shallow dish of heat under a sky of dust. She'd seen only one slough, a green edged wound in the pasture that would disappear in early summer. The idea of being in a place she'd never been before for two months frightened her.

Change was the destroyer. It came in storms that splintered her favorite trees, it came in growth of her favorite calves which led her father to sell them, and it came in crumplings of her grandfather's skin, his wasting in the nursing home.

She pushed her shadow over the gravel and thistles, turned the corner, and went into the Red And White Grocery. In front of her was the particle board post office with its metal wall of 150 post boxes. Sarah shook out her mail key and glanced into the grocery section: lettuce, cabbage, apples, and a few leopard-spotted bananas. She'd have to go into the city soon to get more fruit. The grocer stuck his head around the Cheerio Cornflake corner and grinned at her.

"Good morning there!" he burst out, "And how are you this morning?"

"Good! Very good!" she said too loudly, almost in self defense. She smiled half way behind her hand and tried to think of his name.

"And how is Mrs. Howard?" he said.

"Good, good." She let her eyes stray to post box number 64. The man knew who she was and what she was doing: university student, friend of Suzanne Howard, come to look after old Mrs. Howard in that big empty house for the summer. A few people she'd met had asked her some questions: what church she went to, what classes she was taking, but few remembered her name. She opened the box and found a soft blue envelope. Michael's first letter. At least he knew her. She slid it out of the box. On the back was the return address, "Somewhere in France." She left the grocery and walked back, the sun in her eyes, the wind gusting her hair, the sky sweet and dry in her mouth. She sniffed the envelope, but smelled only cut orange and sour peel on her fingers.

Sarah opened the screen door and stepped into the cool blue-walled air of the kitchen. Ella, still sitting at breakfast, lifted a smile from the edge of her teacup. She sat behind the yellow arborite table and touched her white halo hair with the palm of one hand. She wore a home made house dress, black and white checkered, with a red patch flower on the hip pocket.

Sarah waved the letter and put it on the table. "Nothing for you, but I got one." She tried not to smile. Ella saw.

"Oh . . . do you have a young man?" Ella said, puckering up her smile.

"His name is Michael."

"And he's writing from back home, is he? Where are you from?"

Sarah lifted the teapot lid and saw the minerals in the water crusting on the surface like dirt. She didn't want to answer this question again. "He's writing from Europe. We're both from Saskatoon."

"And what does your father do?"

"He farms. Near Wakaw. I grew up there." Sarah stepped outside to pour the lukewarm tea on the patch of columbine and crabgrass by the step. These were the same questions Ella asked every morning, two, maybe three times. Sarah was homesick enough already, after only a week, and she didn't want to always be reminded. Thinking about home, her parents and her boyfriend, gave her pain, like hunger, in her stomach. She came back inside.

"Do you miss him? Michael?"

"Yes." Sarah half turned, picked up the letter and put it in her shirt pocket. "Do you want to take a walk now, or would you rather have your bath first?"

"Oh . . . the bath I think."

"I'll start running the water, then. I'll be back for you in a couple of minutes."

Sarah went through the dining room, the living room, and up the stairs. She had to ask about the walk, even though she knew Ella probably wouldn't go. They had gone for a walk just after Suzanne left on the first day, when Ella was still quite cheerful. After that, Ella usually said no. On Sunday, Sarah pressed her to go to church, and it was one of the few times when Ella seemed to understand what was happening to her: "I don't want anybody to see me like this, the way I've become." Ella was beginning Alzheimer's disease. Sarah didn't know what to do but let her cry.

Sarah adjusted the taps and dropped a green bath oil marble into the tub. Over the churning water, she heard the stairs creak. She ran out of the bathroom.

"Ella, wait. I'll help you."

The old woman continued up, stepping slowly, leaning one arm on the banister. Her head was motionless, bent down as if she were concentrating on the position of each step, but her eyes were resentful, fixed on Sarah.

"I can climb stairs just fine."

"But Suzanne said you fell on the stairs once last month. Let me —"

"Oh, my granddaughter! What is she trying to do to me? The things she says. I didn't fall. I've never fallen."

There was silence after the groan of each step. Sarah stood, muscles tense, knowing she couldn't be fast enough if Ella stumbled, not knowing whether to give safety at the expense of Ella's self respect. Ella shuffled past her into the bathroom and let the door swing closed. Sarah waited and bit a hangnail until she thought Ella might be undressed, thinking of brittle bird bone, brittle temper.

"Ella? I'll just come in to help you into the tub."

Sarah pushed open the door. Ella was half turned away from her, wearing only a bra.

"I'll unfasten this for you. It's in a pretty hard to get at spot."

Sarah unfastened the bra, then helped Ella climb into the high-sided tub. The first time Sarah had done this, she had been afraid to see Ella's body, afraid to see the wrinkled skin, the sagging breasts. She was surprised when she saw it wasn't much different from her own. It was a mirror. Two arms, two legs, two breasts. Hair where she had hair. It was whole, but still made her uneasy. She remembered getting her first period, how frightened her mother had seemed while describing what changes her body would go through, the parts that would be different. She became as frightened as her mother. Sarah braced her arms on the edge of the tub so Ella could lean on her shoulder as she got in. She watched the old woman to make sure she didn't slip, but she had the urge to close her eyes. She felt Ella's stoop in her own back, felt for the small scabs on her own arms, checked her hands for loose skin and liver spots. Ella got both feet into the tub and lowered herself into the water.

"Is it too hot?"

Ella shook her head.

"I'll be downstairs, so just call when you're ready to come out."

Sarah went to her room to get her walkman and a couple of tapes before going downstairs to do her stretches. She sat on the carpet, took the letter from her pocket, and put it on the floor in front of her. Not yet. She would wait. There was so little to look forward to during the day.

First, the hurdler's stretch. She leaned her face all the way down to the dusty-smelling carpet and held the position. She cranked the music up because it was a good song. It was Michael's tape, the Beatles. He was trying to get her into music from the sixties. She moved her shoulders to the beat and looked around the room. Ella's black and white wedding picture, watercoloured photos of her children at graduation, the very old family picnic picture where Ella is a teenager. Ella said that everyone else in the picture was already dead.

Sarah got up and began to dance. She saw herself in the oval mirror above the writing desk and watched. She stopped, turned the music up again, and stared at herself, the dark eyes, the dark hair falling on her cheeks, the smooth forehead.

"You are not dying," she said.

* * *

Sarah watched the sea gulls wheel over the fields, white sparks in the blue. They knew how to use the wind. She felt a tug in the air and turned to see a dust devil coming off the field beside her. Unable to avoid it, she closed her eyes and let it twist her hair into the dust, into the air, felt the pebbles sting her legs as if she were Dorothy going to Oz. The small tornado left her with a gust and she watched it spin into the stubble across the road and stir more dirt into the air. She was sick of the wind. She didn't mind the sun or the heat, but the wind was always pushing her where she didn't want to go. She got on her bike and rode the straight gravel road back to town.

Ella was sitting at the kitchen table when Sarah got back. In front of her was a plate of crookedly sliced sausage, tomatoes, and bread and butter.

"Oh! I didn't know what happened to you. I didn't know if you were coming back, so I made myself a little something."

"I said I'd be gone only an hour or so, and come back to fix supper."

"Oh, you did?" The old woman's voice was hard, suspicious. "I don't remember that. Sometimes people try to fool an old woman, you know, especially when she lives alone and all."

"I didn't . . . wouldn't . . . " Sarah felt guilty, angry that she had nothing to feel guilty about. How could she stay in the same room with Ella twenty-four hours a day, to listen to how she couldn't follow a story on TV, to how she missed her daughters? Sarah watched Ella pick up a slice of tomato with her fork and eat it, one wet seed swimming out onto her shaking lower lip.

Just after lunch, Sarah had persuaded Ella to walk down the street. They walked the block to the shriveling field of seedling rye, and Ella pointed to the last house, little more than grey wind-battered wood. It was where her best friend once lived, was young, was blown by the wind to old age, to death.

Sarah watched Ella put a piece of sausage in her mouth and chew, then looked down at her own legs, smooth and young, lace-patterned with sunlight through the curtain. She wanted to die before she got as old as Ella, before all her friends had died, before she hadn't enough mind left to visit whoever was remaining.

"Did you say where you were from?" Ella smiled at her, rubbing bread crumbs off her fingers.

"Saskatoon."

Sarah went out the screen door and leaned against the house, the sun hot on her eyes, squinting at the crab apple tree that had once snowed its blossoms onto the lawn. She looked at her hands and saw the dry little cracks at a few of the fingertips. The wind had cracked them. Her hands were beginning to look like her mother's.

* * *

There wasn't rain, so she made her own in the evening. She sat on a kitchen chair she'd pulled onto the patio, listening to the sprinkler, smelling the wet earth, the dust washing from the leaves in the deep blue garden. It was the loneliest time, the time when even the sun left her. She opened the letter and held the pages in the window light.

She looked for him in the letter, and she looked for herself. The first paragraphs were only chateaux and cathedrals and gardens. The last paragraph started with him, then was about her — no, about her body. Bits and pieces of it. Her breasts and the part between her legs, the red-brown lips and the deep inside, the part she hadn't yet allowed him to touch or even see. She was afraid. She thought she was too young, and she wanted to stay too young. He should have known that. She re-read,

angry. How could he think she wanted to hear this? Cathedrals
and chateaux and her body like a landscape — but only the parts
he found most interesting. She read the letter again and couldn't
find herself in it. He didn't know her. She reached down, turned
off the tap, and the rain stopped. She walked into the kitchen
and saw Ella, blue nightgowned and barefoot, unplugging the
toaster.

"What are you doing awake?"

Ella looked up, lips pinched, eyes frightened. "I don't want
any fires in the walls. The wires, you know. I don't know why
you don't unplug these." Her lips relaxed, then her forehead
knotted in confusion. "I — I woke up on the couch."

Sarah went to her. "It's okay. I put some sheets there for you
because it's too hot upstairs." She led Ella back to the living
room and helped her crawl between the sheets. The small
electric fan on the floor was also unplugged. "The fan will keep
you cool. Are you sure you don't want it?"

Ella looked up and shook her head. Fires in the walls. She
smiled and the light reflected in her watery hazel eyes: sparks
bright as gulls over the sand blown fields. Sarah sat and took
the old woman in her arms, pressing her face into the white
dandelion hair. She felt the small bird arms around her shoulders, and was surprised at their strength, surprised at how solid
Ella's body felt. "Good night."

"Good night. You know, sometimes I think you look a little
like Suzanne, my granddaughter. Do you know her?"

"Yes."

Ella slid down and turned away to put her head on the
pillow. Sarah looked up at the pictures of Ella's children and
grandchildren, the parts of Ella's body, before she got up to
turn off the light. She walked upstairs in the dark, pushing into
the hot air that hung at the top of the house. After washing the

heat off her face and arms in the bathroom sink, she went to her bedroom.

Naked under the sheet, she was still too hot. She had never slept without some sort of covering, but she threw the sheet off like a wave and pushed the last ripples to the edge of the bed so nothing was touching her. It was all right: she didn't feel exposed. The light from the street slanted through the window onto the old, water-wrinkled ceiling, the ceiling pressed against the air against her body. After only a week, she knew the ceiling, every wrinkle, like she knew her body.

Tomorrow, she would walk hand in hand with an old woman instead of a young man. Before she went to sleep, she imagined how she'd look with white hair, white like the crab apple trees in spring, snowing blossoms like falling sunlight, the sun pushing the wind.

THE SEASONS ARE HORSES

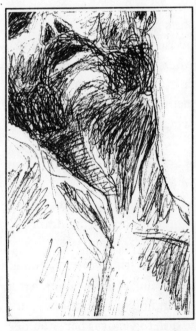

Yellow leaves clatter around Pablo's hooves as we gallop toward the fence, and his muscles bunch as if he's going to kick off the ground. I pull back, but there's still a second when he's in the air. Partly, that's just the way horses are: people shouldn't expect them to keep touching the ground. Why else would artists paint them with wings? You only have to fly once to know you can do it forever.

Mom comes over to the corral in her town shoes, wearing one of those shirts that cover your hips if your hips are too big. Her upper lip curls and shows her teeth like when she's trying to please Dad. It's sort of a smile, but not really. Her eyes are linered blue and purple, but it's too dark, like she's getting ready to cry bruises. It's strange. Her makeup is always just right, even when she's not going out anywhere. Dad wants her to look the way she did when she went to church and meant it. She told me she doesn't love God no more, and you know, neither do I, Him going around, playing with His power, making people miserable. When I was small, she would make me beautiful for church, too, even put pearl nail polish on me, and tell me I had such pretty hands. She'd be angry then, and tell me her hands were ugly. I hated myself for that. I don't want to be beautiful.

She puts her foot on the bottom pole of the fence like she's getting ready to climb over. I ride up. Pablo's already in a sweat, but he wants to go more, maybe try the mud fields and the slough.

"Fall already," she says, as if she's got nothing to say. I liked it when she used to come out and ride with me. We wouldn't say much. We'd just be together. But that hasn't happened in a long time, not with her running away to town so much, sometimes even after supper, sometimes Dad almost killing her when she comes back. I hate it when she's gone. Dad expects more from me when she's gone.

"Going to Grassbank," she says. "You want some pop? You got almost none left. I'll get you a 6-pack."

Pablo shakes and stamps under me. "Yeah, sure. You going to be gone long?" I say, knowing my eyes are saying don't go, don't go.

She looks at me, hopeless, as if she's hearing horses running, and they're running right over her. I think of Dad calling her a lazy godless harlot. I think of her standing in the doorway, her apron tied around her middle, the dish towel over her shoulder like a harness.

"Could be a while in town," she says finally, fumbling, trying to close her purse. I think she's drunk. She reaches out to touch Pablo and he jerks away.

"He doesn't like me, Selina," she says, and then turns around quick, like she does when she doesn't want me or the boys to see her cry. I think she's crazy, maybe. When I was little and the boys weren't born yet, Dad sometimes took us for ice cream after church, even before we'd had lunch. Dad would have his arm around me, tease me and call me his girlfriend, and Mom would be sitting across from us, tissue tucked neatly around her cone to catch the drips, letting the tears run down her cheeks. Dad would hold me tighter and take licks off my ice cream.

She walks away through the puddles like she doesn't notice the mud sliming up the toes of her good shoes. When she opens the door of the pick-up, I see her travel bag on the passenger seat. She gets in.

"Get you your favorites," she calls through the window. "Pepsi and grape. Okay?"

I'm surprised she doesn't tell me to get back in the house and watch Raymie and Cody. Dad doesn't like me fooling with the horses much when I could be doing work in the house.

The wheels spin mud over the sidewalk and I watch the brake lights flash when she gets out to the highway. She honks when she drives past Mona Littlechild's place just inside the reserve. Dad always tells her not to go by the reserve road, but to go the extra two miles around.

I keep watching the highway. Lyle is coming to pick me up in a half-hour. I jump down and lead Pablo into the barn, take off his saddle and bridle, and give him a rub down. When I come out, Lyle's truck is already waiting at Mona's. He can't come here. Dad swears he'll run him off. Lyle and Mona are cousins.

We go to Lyle's basement place in Grassbank. He says when we get married he's going to get a better job, better place. He flops on the carpet and pulls out a plastic bag. "Guess what I've got," he says.

Hash. I don't like it. I don't say anything because Lyle is twenty-one and I'm sixteen and feel I don't know enough to complain. Besides, free country.

He gets ready and lies back on my lap. He likes me to take care of him. Soon, he's not there anymore, inside his body, and I feel there's no point in me being here. It was better at first, when everything was new. Lyle used to draw me pictures of unicorns. He used to take me to Saskatoon and we'd go to movies and eat bags and bags of popcorn. He used to make me believe I was beautiful, even though every day I looked in the mirror and saw my stringy brown hair, skinny arms, and zits. He's very still and I stroke his black hair. He did a lot this time because he needs a bigger kick. That's what he calls it anyway. I tried it a few times. The only reason it's good is you don't have to think or do anything anymore, but if that's what you want, you may as well be dead.

I go out and get us a couple of videos and we watch until I want to sleep and go home at the same time. He comes halfway out of the trip and wants to do it. We don't have anything, not even a baggie or nothing I joke, but he doesn't laugh. We do it and I don't know whether I want to or not. I think of God punishing me like he sends the depression on Dad, and the rain this harvest. I think of the pills Dad threw in the garbage because rye worked just as good and he didn't need a prescription for it. I think of Dad, lying on top of me. Maybe God is punishing me already. I figured it didn't matter if I did it with Lyle. I've got nothing to save for marriage anyway, but maybe I was wrong. God can always punish you more. There's always Hell, or — a kid. Oh, God.

"Lyle, we going to have a kid now?" I say, but he laughs.

"It won't be a red man or a white man. It'll be pink! Or at least tan." He holds me and I shut my eyes. I shut my eyes all the way home in the truck.

He drops me off at the driveway and I walk the dark road, the gravel sharp under my shoes. It's cold and clouds cover the stars. The horses can smell me and walk beside me behind the barbed wire, making little talking noises in their throats. They don't do this for Dad, even when he's got carrots.

The pick-up isn't by the fuel tanks where it usually is. I think of Mom's travel bag. The yard light sparks with moths and casts big shadows, not big enough to hide a truck.

"So where is she?" Dad says, after I come in. He's standing by the kitchen sink and he can see the whole living room because he knocked the wall down last year after he put a couple of holes in it with a chair. He's got a bottle opener in his hand, still in his grease-soaked field clothes, one eye half open as if part of his brain is gone.

When he's like this, sometimes I don't answer because it doesn't make a difference whether I do or not. I wish it was morning. Some mornings, when he's dried out, he smiles when the eggs and bacon are done just right. He even laughs on mornings when it's not raining.

I pick up the newspapers and the God magazines off the sofa. The house has to be clean when Dad wakes up in the morning. Cody should be in bed, but he's reading wrestling magazines. My hands shake. Maybe there's a baby inside me already. I got no control. If a baby starts, you can't tell your body what to do no more.

Dad leans against the kitchen counter to watch me.

"You know where she is," he growls and I can smell whatever it is that's made him drunk. His head sags to the side. "She tells you things, doesn't she? She tells you what it's like to be with *him*."

I don't look. I start putting the supper dishes in the sink and filling it with water.

"Selina!"

"She went to town about three-thirty. Took the pick-up. I think she might be a long time," I mumble, keeping my eyes down. I throw the dish towel over my shoulder, get the rest of the dishes off the table, and look at all the beer bottles there. I put on one of Mom's blank faces, the one that says there's nothing inside her but what he tells her.

"Doesn't matter what you think. You could have stopped her. She's going around, the whore, showing everybody what a fool I am. And you know who she's with? The pick-up was parked right outside his place for everyone to see!" He looks around for something to kill, and swipes the dishes off the counter. They're the non-breakable kind, so most of them clatter around on the floor, but one explodes into a million jagged pebbles. "Conrad Siemens. That's who your mother is screwing around with."

Conrad. His second cousin. The guy who works at the hardware in town.

Dad comes toward me, work boots crunching on the glass.

"Cody, you go to bed now," I say, quiet, keeping still. I don't want him to get it, too. I don't want him to even see it, but he just stays there, hanging on to the sofa.

Dad grabs my arm and I see the blood webs in his eyes before his fist explodes onto my ear. I tear away from him and stumble over to the arm chair, covering my head with my hands. I think about the times Mom ran with us to the shelter in Saskatoon, and Dad had come, crying and begging, saying it would never happen again. Mom always believed him, and he took us out for ice cream like he used to when he owned the land instead of renting it. I think of the little tan baby that could be inside me, and of me alone on the outside, nothing but fists around me. I hear Cody starting to cry.

"Just shut up," Dad says, and starts toward him. He pulls Cody off the sofa and slaps the side of his head. I can't take it, Cody whimpering. Maybe it's the devil that comes into me, and picks me off the chair. I grab the bread knife from the table.

"You just stay away from us, you hear?" I say, and cut the air in front of his face. "Because I'll kill you. I'll kill you." Dad backs away, eyes wide. Cody runs behind me.

"You crazy bitch." He's white, like that day he came back from the bank with next to nothing.

I grab Cody by the sweater, holding the knife up like a cross. We back down the hallway, get inside the boys' room and close the door with a chair. Raymie is small and shivering in the big bed. Something bangs against the door: fists, curses. We get under the covers and the boys put their small arms around my middle, the three of us together, maybe four. The knife is on the bed. There's the sound of rain on the window, and then Dad outside, screaming at the storm.

* * *

I look out the kitchen window and see the horses walking along the fence, like they're waiting for me to open the gate. The dishwater is cold by the time I put the last pot in the rack, and I pull the plug. I can't get Mom's apron off. It's knotted over the small of my back, and I pick and pull at the knot until I can't stand it and tear one of the ties off. I go to the bathroom, pull down my jeans and look for blood on my panties. Nothing. I don't even bother putting a pad there anymore. I was supposed to be on the rag a week ago just like Mom was supposed to come back that night, three weeks ago. The mirror shows how grey I look, how grey I feel. I look like Mom after one of Dad's bad nights, without the bruises and the makeup to hide behind. I hear a truck in the yard and go out on the porch. Cody and Raymie are already there.

It's the pick-up. It's her. She slams the truck door and it sounds hollow, like a steel drum, only there's Conrad inside. He gets out, walking with his arms hanging tense, looking around, ready to fight if he has to. He looks at Mom, worried, the sun shining on his blonde hair.

"It's all right. You better stay here for now," she says to him. She gets a box out of the back of the truck and comes toward the house. Raymie drops his doll, the one I gave him, and runs to her like she was dead and now she's alive.

"Mom! Mom!"

Cody hangs back with me. We don't trust her. She comes to the porch, slides the box onto the top step while we look down at her, and picks up Raymie.

"Where were you?" he says, in his small, hurting voice.

She bites her lip. She's not wearing any makeup and her cheeks are white as bread, but she doesn't look beaten. The wrinkles are soft and tender around her eyes.

"Oh, look Raymie. See what Mommy brought you?"

Tears break up her voice. In the box are chocolate bars, a coloring book, a wrestling magazine, and two six packs of pop. Pepsi and grape. Damn long shopping trip to bring back nothing but junk.

"That's all?" I say.

She doesn't say anything, doesn't tell me to shut my mouth, so she seems unreal. I want her to try to boss me, the way she used to, just try me and see.

"Mona phoned me," she says quietly. "Said Dad was out combining on the south quarter? Is that right? Is he gone?"

So she wants me to be her spy, too. You can't see the south quarter from the house, so if he's there, she's safe. I don't want her to be safe.

"Why did you go?" Cody says. There's this slapped look on his face, slapped for something he didn't do. She puts Raymie down and he hangs on to her leg like she might fly away.

"I'm sorry," she says.

"Sure you are." I pick up the Pepsi and let it drop on the sidewalk. One of the cans explodes and spews brown fizz on the cement.

"I phoned. He wouldn't let me talk to you. And don't you talk to me like that."

"I'll do whatever the hell I please."

"I don't think so."

I jerk the whole box off the step and Raymie gasps when he sees his coloring book soaking up a puddle gone rancid with leaves.

"What do you want with that anyway?" I scream at him. "She doesn't give a damn about you!"

Mom stands there, her mouth open, her eyes shut, her breath stopped. I listen to the horse we shut up in the barn this morning, waiting for the vet. He's kicking the splinters out of his stall.

"I'm going to get Dad."

"No, Selina."

I run across the yard, thinking about how I've got her now. She'll stay. Dad will make her. When I get to the trail road through the bush, I run like she's right behind, going to pass me and pull the gate shut in front of me, and nothing will be the same again. Not anything.

I can hardly breathe when I get through the bush and see the combine on the other side of the field, chawing grain stalks and spinning out clouds of chaff. I keep running, listening to my breath, my feet hitting the ground, the stubble, the swaths.

Dad stops the combine, pulls a lever, and the dragging, wide jaws lift up, still chewing. He sticks his head out the door.

"What the hell are you doing, running on my swaths? Can't you see the rain's ruined them enough?"

"I — sorry." He hasn't touched us since that night with the knife, though he beats us more with words — when he's around.

Mostly, he's in the barn, on the field, at the bar. "Who's taking care of the boys if you're not?"

"Mom. Mom's here." I say, breathless. "He's with her."

He comes out and stands at the top of the ladder, standing like God with dirt on his face.

"Tell her to go to hell."

He drops the jaw of the combine and it roars away. I walk back through the bush.

Maybe Dad's right. She doesn't want us, well, we don't want her. On Mona's yard, the laundry is out. It hangs, mostly long sleeved shirts, like animal hides. Mona's house has no yard, but was pitched in the meadow, and the cars herd around it like ponies, like she could leave any old time. Lyle drives up in his truck. He gets out and waves. I wave back and walk up to the house. Mom and Conrad are looting it — mostly her clothes. As if I cared.

"Selina, wait a minute."

"You didn't."

"I want to talk to you. There's something you have to know."

She follows me all the way to the bathroom and I slam the door and lock it.

"Please come out and talk to me."

I pull everything down. My panties are white, like everything is pure and good and nobody ever hurts or bleeds or cries.

"I don't need this," I yell through the door. "I don't need you like you don't need us. I'm getting out of here." I zip up my jeans and open the door. She's standing right there.

"You're going with Lyle, aren't you? He's over at Mona's."

I lift my head high. She can't stop me. She's looking at me like she knows it.

"Don't do it, Selina. It'll be the same thing all over again so you won't be getting away. Lyle gets stoned just like Dad gets drunk." She leans against the wall. "Your dad, he used to say

all the right things, you know. He'd sit beside me in church like
he was really listening, and later, after the wedding, I found out
all he heard was the obey part. Can you see? I can't do this
anymore. You've got to live for yourself sometime."

"What about the boys?"

She doesn't answer and doesn't look at me. "You can come
with me," she says, quiet.

"What about the boys?"

"We can't. We just can't." She's crying. "I don't even know
if he'll let you go, but you have to get away."

I push past her and go out the back door so I don't have to
see Cody and Ramie. How could I go without the boys? How
could I leave Lyle with his little tan baby growing inside me?

I go out to the corral and stare at Lyle's truck over at Mona's.
I think of getting the breakfast that morning, of getting the boys
up, of holding Lyle when he's stoned, of protecting Cody from
Dad, of always taking care of someone else. I think of how long
it's been since I've ridden — three weeks. The seasons are horses
running away from you.

I saddle up Pablo. Mom and Conrad are gone when I get out
of the barn, and I figure Lyle can take care of himself if he wants
to get stoned today. I mount and hold Pablo back. There's this
stabbing in my stomach and crotch. I see horses, their hooves
not touching the ground, flying. I give Pablo a kick because I'm
going to fly over the fence with him. I will fly so wild, the blood
will flow out of me, down his back.